D1517223

THE SEMESTER OF
OUR DISCONTENT

This Large Print Book carries the
Seal of Approval of N.A.V.H.

THE SEMESTER OF OUR DISCONTENT

CYNTHIA KUHN

THORNDIKE PRESS
A part of Gale, a Cengage Company

Farmington Hills, Mich • San Francisco • New York • Waterville, Maine
Meriden, Conn • Mason, Ohio • Chicago

St. John the Baptist Parish Library
2920 New Hwy. 51
LaPlace, LA 70068

Copyright © 2016 by Cynthia Kuhn.
Thorndike Press, a part of Gale, a Cengage Company.

ALL RIGHTS RESERVED
This is a work of fiction. Any references to historical events, to real people, or to real locales are used fictitiously. Other names, characters, places, and incidents are the product of the author's imagination and any resemblance to actual events or locales or person, living or dead, is entirely coincidental.
Thorndike Press® Large Print Clean Reads.
The text of this Large Print edition is unabridged.
Other aspects of the book may vary from the original edition.
Set in 16 pt. Plantin.

LIBRARY OF CONGRESS CIP DATA ON FILE.
CATALOGUING IN PUBLICATION FOR THIS BOOK
IS AVAILABLE FROM THE LIBRARY OF CONGRESS

ISBN-13: 978-1-4328-4879-8 (hardcover)

Published in 2018 by arrangement with Henery Press, LLC

Printed in the United States of America
1 2 3 4 5 6 7 22 21 20 19 18

For my family

ACKNOWLEDGMENTS

Thank you to the following . . .

Kendel Lynn, Erin George, Rachel Jackson, Anna Davis, Art Molinares, and everyone at Henery Press — for taking a chance on me, for making the book better, and for being amazing and fabulous all around. And the authors in the Hen House — for being so welcoming and helpful.

Metropolitan State University of Denver — for the sabbatical during which the manuscript was finished. Also for the opportunity to work with so many terrific colleagues and students.

Harriette Sackler and everyone at Malice Domestic — for the honor and assistance of The William F. Deeck-Malice Domestic Grant for Unpublished Writers (of mystery).

Sisters in Crime, Camp NaNo Guppy

Cabin, Club Herky people, and Mysteristas both past and present — for community and inspiration.

James Aubrey, Maggie Barbieri, Ellen Byron, Theresa Crater, Carman Curton, Laura DiSilverio, Sandra Maresh Doe, Sebastian Doherty, Margarita Barceló Flores, Erin Webster Garrett, Elsie Haley, Nancy Hightower, Lorna Hutchison, Sybil Johnson, Mylee Khristoforov, Catriona McPherson, Jason Miller, Josie and Stuart Mills, Mikkilynn Olmsted, Keenan Powell, Lori Rader-Day, Lev Raphael, Christy and Bob Rowe, Renée Ruderman, Gene Saxe, Megan Springate, Mary Sutton, Craig Svonkin, Dana Talusani, and last but certainly not least, Diane Vallere — for your readings, generous words, and/or other much-appreciated kindnesses.

William and Dorothy Guerrera; Wendy, Seth, Jackson, and Charlie Crichton; Sue Crichton; Shawn and James Peterka; Willard Crichton; Dennis, Ursula, Gretchen, Grant, Brianna, Allie, Eric, Amelia, Karl, and Meg Kuhn — for your encouragement and support. Special thanks to my father for coming up with the perfect character name (Lexington) on a dime, to my mother and husband for being earliest readers, to my brother-in-law for being a later reader, and to my sister for not only reading but also listening, cheering, and making me laugh when I needed it most over the years.

Finally, to Kenneth, Griffin, and Sawyer Kuhn — for far more than I could ever list. You are my sunshine. Deepest gratitude and love.

CHAPTER 1

When summoned by the department chair, one shows up on time. I hurried past the row of faculty mailboxes with minutes to spare and greeted Millicent Quayle, a squarish middle-aged woman whose dull brown hair perfectly matched her suit. As executive assistant, Millicent presided over the front desk that guarded our leader's inner sanctum. She was practically humming with efficiency as her fingers flew over the keyboard, and I stood quietly until she mustered up the will to drag her attention away from the computer screen.

"And you are?" She frowned, her eyes locked on mine.

"I'm Lila," I reminded her. "New professor? Dr. Higgins wanted to see me."

Not even a blink. I had the fleeting impression she was expecting me to curtsy.

I did not.

Millicent slowly consulted an appointment

calendar with gilded edges and made a small check in the page margin. "He's with someone right now. Please take a seat," she said, waving at the upholstered chair by the window. As I complied, she returned to her work.

I gazed across campus towards the wrought-iron gates flanked by a pair of granite gryphons that marked the main entrance. It was an imposing entry, intentionally so. Officially, Stonedale University offered a "liberal arts education to a small number of exceptionally qualified students." Unofficially, it was known as an exclusive school for those who didn't make it into the Ivy League but who were, according to their parents at least, exceptional nonetheless.

Nestled into the foothills southwest of Denver, Stonedale's location was very popular with students. While the administration was more inclined to celebrate the university's curricular rigor and high rankings, part of the appeal for students was its proximity to Rocky Mountain hiking, skiing, and snowboarding. Another selling feature for parents and students alike was the air of sanctuary offered by the campus. Charming stone buildings with all manner of architectural flourishes clustered around a burbling fountain, and numerous tall trees contributed to the sense of being enclosed in a protective haven. There were other structures radiating outward from the main circle, but they were never featured in any of the recruiting publications. This, what we all called "the green," was the carefully calibrated and highly picturesque heart of Stonedale.

Voices rising in the chair's office — muffled, but clearly irate — paused my reflections. The door flew open and my colleague Tad Ruthersford stormed out, his face flushed. He shot me an unreadable look as he departed.

Roland Higgins emerged soon after, carrying a large book. He seemed to be unpleasantly damp from the effort. Or perhaps from the tweed — who wore such a heavy fabric in September?

"File this." He slammed the text onto Millicent's desk. I had to give her credit. She didn't flinch at the loud sound, just pulled open the side drawer of her desk with one hand and swept the offending volume inside with the other.

Catching sight of me, Roland froze, peering through his greasy rimless glasses, which I was certain he would have referred to as "spectacles." After an extended pause, his mouth moved. "You're here."

I agreed.

He stared at me long past the point of politeness, then turned to Millicent. "Faculty meeting today . . . what time?"

"The usual time," she replied.

"Two?" he asked, wrinkling his nose in distaste. "But it's almost one already. What a nuisance. I have important work to finish. Don't you?" He glowered at me, as if I were responsible for scheduling the imposition.

"Yes," I said, practically whispering in the face of Roland's displeasure. He patted his thick thighs a few times as he let his disapproval sink in. With his black suit and white shirt, flapping with exasperation, he looked like an indignant penguin.

"Come in," he said, finally.

I followed him into the stifling mausoleum of a room, which was dim aside from an ineffective reading lamp perched on the mahogany desk. If the shades were jolted open, a tidal wave of dust would surely rise and consume us both. Roland indicated I should take the skeletal chair facing his desk while he lowered himself into a brown leather executive number on the other side. Once we were both situated, he shuffled through the materials cluttering the surface until he located a stapled packet.

"I read your special topics course proposal. The curriculum chair shared it with me." He held the pages at the corner with two fingers, as if they were contagious. "We hired you to teach American literature and the occasional Gothic course, Dr. Maclean. Not mystery."

"Right, but Gothic and mystery overlap —"

He went on as if I hadn't said anything. "I know you've only been here a few weeks, Dr. Maclean, but new professors do not propose courses. We prefer that junior faculty members better acquaint themselves with our program first. Especially those fresh out of graduate school."

I chose to ignore the unmistakable message about knowing my place. "I was reading through the curriculum to acquaint myself, actually, and noticed there weren't any literature courses on mystery, so . . ." I gestured to the packet.

Roland leaned back in the chair and steepled his fingers. "There's a reason for that, isn't there?"

I conjured up a confused expression, though I already knew where he was headed. "What *is* the reason?"

He seemed surprised, either by the question or the fact that I had dared to ask it. "Dr. Maclean, our courses celebrate *major* works. Authors and texts who have made a lasting contribution to literature. Certainly you know the difference."

"I know that even conservative definitions would include —"

Roland cleared his throat, smoothed his tie patterned with fire-breathing dragons, and launched into a diatribe about literature's universal values. During the lecture, he closed his eyes — all the better to avoid pesky interruptions. While he belabored his arguments, the gray mustache curved over his mouth like a misplaced comma nobly rode out the torrent of words. At the conclusion of his tirade, Roland looked at me expectantly.

"Ah," I said.

He inclined his head ever so slightly, as if he were a king granting me a great favor.

A moment passed.

"But —" I began.

"It's a question of significance," he said. "This proposal will not be forwarded. It's not the right time for you to do this."

A drop of perspiration rolled down my ribcage. "Would it be better if one of my colleagues proposed it?"

He lurched forward in the chair and snapped, "I repeat, it's not time for you to do this."

"But isn't it time for someone to do this? Most universities include popular —"

Roland's face grew red and his jowls quivered. "Stonedale is not like other universities. We have our own way of doing things. Period." He pointed at me. "And let me be direct, while we're at it. As a rule, junior faculty members need to talk less and listen more."

"What?" I sat up straighter.

"In meetings and so forth. You'll find your senior colleagues have much to teach you."

Of course they did. But was he really telling me not to speak?

Roland drummed his fingers on the desktop.

I lifted my chin and met his gaze. "You want me to be quiet until I have tenure?"

He narrowed his eyes. "If you *are* ever tenured. You have six years of reappointment to get through first."

That shut me up.

"Speaking of which, Dr. Maclean, I have some concerns about your research. How is your project progressing?"

"Well . . ." I paused. I'd been so consumed by the demands of teaching that I hadn't been able to accomplish much writing yet. But as I tried to formulate a truthful answer that didn't make me sound like a slacker, he kept going.

"Remind me what you are working on," he commanded.

I shifted gears into a well-rehearsed-in-grad-school plan for making the literary world more aware of an unknown mystery writer named Isabella Dare.

"Fine," Roland barked. "That's enough."

He had, since our first encounter, made it apparent that he viewed my choice of an author unfamiliar to him as an intentional affront. I still hadn't figured out the appropriate response. Actually, I'm not sure there was one, other than to suggest he try having a more open mind now and then, which wouldn't go over well.

"I'm still not convinced your topic will be productive enough to meet anyone's expectations. You do have to publish, you know."

I forced myself to sit perfectly still as he continued.

"However, I know you worked with Avery Lane on your dissertation. Although I question her decision to allow you to center your research on such a — let's say *unproven* — writer, I do know she will have been most stringent in her supervision of your work. Did she mention we have a bit of history?"

"Just that you'd studied at Yale together." I omitted the part about Roland being a pompous ass on a power trip. She had been very clear on that point.

"Avery is a remarkable scholar," he said, almost meditatively, while his eyes wandered to a point somewhere behind my left ear. "If she hadn't called me to sing your praises, you probably wouldn't be sitting here."

I wasn't about to respond to the implications of *that.*

"Focusing a dissertation on a woman whose work has not been written about before is risky, isn't it?" He smirked.

"I think she's important. Avery encouraged me and convinced the rest of the committee —"

"She's always been persuasive. If Avery thinks highly of you and your topic, I suppose we shall have to keep that in mind." He jerked his head at the door. I gladly walked through it and away from him.

Calista James was waiting outside. In her sleeveless beaded silver dress, she could have been a 1920s flapper. On most people, it would have seemed like a Halloween costume, but it suited the poet, who was my cousin as well as my colleague. There was no visible family resemblance between us — she was blonde and shortish whereas I was brunette and tallish; her hair was

19

straight, mine was wavy; her eyes were gray, mine green. However, we did share an inclination to blurt things out at unfortunate times and a disinclination to suffer injustices quietly, both of which had gotten us into plenty of trouble as we were growing up.

"What was that about?" She gestured me over, the beads on her dress set flailing by the vigorous motions, and pulled me in the opposite direction.

We passed several closed office doors and bulletin boards bursting with multicolored flyers, keeping our voices low.

"Roland didn't like the mystery course I submitted. Also, he thinks I'm not acting appropriately 'junior' as a faculty member."

Her eyes widened. "Seriously? What did you say to him?"

I recounted the entire conversation.

"Brava," Calista said. "Takes most people years to muster up the courage to confront Roland. You stood up to him already."

"I don't know about that. I just tried to state facts. Mostly."

Calista laughed. "Roland does not like hearing facts. He likes giving lectures. And plenty of them."

"He definitely lectured me."

"Was it as boring as it was long-winded?" she asked, smoothing her sharply angled platinum bob. "And as offensive as it was outdated?"

"Indeed."

She grinned at me, the spitting image of my beloved aunt.

"How long do you have to be here before you can propose a course?" I asked her.

"Technically, whenever you like," she said.

"Didn't seem like it. Roland practically called me a whippersnapper. Hasn't anyone proposed a special topics course on popular culture before?"

"Many times."

"So why aren't there any? It's unfathomable in this day and age."

Calista sighed. "Blame it on the system. The chair must sign the forms before they go to the next level, and Roland blocks whatever he wants. It doesn't matter if the curriculum committee approves a proposal or not. It's outrageous, really. If I'd known you were working on a proposal, I would have filled you in."

"It's okay," I said. "But didn't you have a meeting with Roland today too? What happened?"

"Oh, that." She waved it off. "I need to gather some notes before the faculty meeting, so I'll have to tell you later."

She gave me a quick hug before zooming

away. I marveled at her energy level. Calista had always been able to do things faster than the rest of us mere mortals.

Maybe if I walked fast enough, I could escape the dark cloud Roland had just positioned above my head.

Twenty minutes before the meeting was scheduled to begin, my assigned faculty mentor Judith Westerly popped her head into my office. In an impeccably tailored teal suit, her long white hair swept back in a complicated twist, she put me in mind of an Alfred Hitchcock heroine — cool, collected, and highly capable. She had been at Stonedale for almost thirty years and was an adept guide so far. I especially appreciated the fact that she seemed genuinely glad I was here.

We exchanged pleasantries, and she consulted her dainty gold watch. "Perhaps we should head to the faculty meeting? It's a little early — we all try to avoid it until the last possible minute, of course — but that means we would have our choice of seats and could settle in before all the hubbub. I'll show you the best vantage points."

I followed her into the hallway, pulled the door shut behind me, and locked it.

"Truth be told, I'm not in a hurry to

return to the departmental agenda," said Judith as we walked. "At the last meeting of spring term, we spent two hours arguing over the font on our letterhead. Can you believe it? Then the deadlock over Arial and Helvetica went on for another week in an email battle."

"Which font won?" I asked.

"That's the whole point. It was tabled to be revisited this fall." She smiled. "You may be the tiebreaker, Lila."

"No thanks," I said. The last thing I wanted to do was antagonize half of the department.

"Don't worry. It will be a blind vote. We don't want to put you in any uncomfortable situations."

"That's nice of you."

"Not at first, anyway," she added with a wink.

We arrived at the arched entrance to the department library. The intricately carved wooden door swung open slowly when I pushed on it, though the hinges protested loudly.

At the sight of the lifeless form sprawled across the conference table, I shrieked and Judith gasped. One of the fiery dragons on Roland's elegant tie had been slashed in half by the knife embedded in his chest.

CHAPTER 2

About an hour later, Judith and I waited, as we'd been directed to do, in the second-floor hallway. There was quite a crowd working the department library — both campus and Stonedale police had representatives upstairs, as well as crime scene investigators — and they'd moved us out of the way. Police personnel down here were clustered, talking in low voices. The adrenaline surging through my veins had dulled to weariness, and my head was starting to throb. For all I knew, Roland's killer was lurking around a corner somewhere, yet I felt strangely disconnected, numb. Perhaps I was still in shock.

Among the many horrors to be encountered at an English department meeting, a dead body was not usually one of them. I had been prepared for the standard litany of complaints, the political jousting, the barely audible snarling — but not this.

I looked at Judith. "How are you doing?"
She shook her head.

I repositioned myself in the student desk — awful contraptions, yoking together uncomfortable chairs and inadequate writing trays, which seems like a failure on both fronts — and stared at the opposite wall until the door to one of the classrooms opened.

A somber-faced man with sharp cheekbones and a buzz cut stepped outside, the badge on his belt catching the light for a moment. "Thanks, ladies, for your patience. I'm Detective Archer. I need to speak with you, one at a time." He glanced down at the notepad in his hand that was open vertically, reporter-style. "Starting with Liza Maclean."

I stood up immediately.

"It's Lila."

"Sorry about that," he said, scowling at the paper and slamming the cover closed. "Please follow me." I did, noting the way the navy suit jacket pulled tight across his back and strained against the muscles of his upper arms. The dark hair along the back of his neck was cut in a straight line. He was the kind of guy you'd see playing a Secret Service agent in the movies: neatly contained but clearly dangerous.

Leading me into a classroom, he folded himself into a desk and pointed to another that had been turned to face his. "Take a seat." He pulled out a tape recorder and held it up for me to inspect. "Okay if I use this?" When I agreed, he pressed the play button. "Detective Lexington Archer, Stonedale P.D., September fourth at 2:57 p.m. Interview with Lila Maclean." He caught my eye. "May I have your permission to tape this conversation?"

"Yes."

He handed back the driver's license an officer had taken from me earlier. "You're thirty? That's young for a professor, isn't it?"

"Not if you go right through," I said. "I didn't take any time off after undergrad."

He nodded thoughtfully.

"If you don't mind my saying so, you look a little young to be a detective too." I'd have pegged him as late thirties, maybe early forties.

His mouth quirked. "I'm old enough, I promise." He flipped open his notepad and positioned the pen over a blank page. "Do you prefer Professor or Doctor?"

"Either. Or neither." It was the first time anyone had ever asked me that. I didn't even know the answer myself.

"Most of the professors I've met prefer one or the other."

"Formality can make a difference in the way people treat you in higher education. Not that I agree with that." With concerted effort, I managed to stop myself from further lamenting the complexities of academic culture. "Please call me Lila, Detective Archer."

"Got it. What is your position here?"

"Assistant professor of English."

He began making notes. "Have you been in Stonedale long?"

"Four weeks. This is my first semester."

His pen moved busily across the page. "Where were you before that?"

"New York."

"City?"

"Yes. I graduated from NYU last spring."

He circled something. I couldn't imagine what in that brief exchange deserved emphasis. As I tried to stretch my neck unobtrusively for a better vantage point, Detective Archer shifted so I couldn't see his notepad.

"Tell me about the events of this afternoon," he said.

"Judith Westerly and I went to the department library to attend the faculty meeting."

"What time was this?" His pen was hovering over his notepad again.

"Quarter to two."

"Did you touch anything in the room?"

"No. I was only in there for a minute or so."

"What did you see when you walked in?"

"The man."

The detective waited.

"And the knife."

He said nothing. His silence was disconcerting.

"And the blood." The memory of that dark pool dripping slowly onto the carpet triggered my gag reflex. I grasped the side of the desk to steady myself and took a few deep breaths.

Archer cleared his throat. "Right. Did you recognize the man?"

"Oh. It was Roland Higgins."

"Did you know him?"

"Yes. He was my department chair."

"What was your impression of him?"

"He was very knowledgeable about his area," I said, trying to keep it professional.

"I mean as a person. What was he like?"

I hesitated.

"Roland had a big personality. He liked to make his presence known."

"Can you elaborate on that?"

"He had definite opinions about certain

things and was rude to anyone who disagreed with him."

"For example?" he prodded, pen poised.

I sorted through potential options in my mind while gazing at the classroom's white board behind Archer, covered with the ghostly remains of unintelligible class notes. "I guess I would say he was overly concerned with tradition."

The detective made some more notes. "What do you mean by tradition?"

"A single literary tradition. The idea that there are only certain writers who deserve to be studied — mostly 'dead white men.' "

His head snapped up. "Is that a *joke*?"

"No," I said, blushing. "Just . . . unfortunate terminology, given the circumstances."

Archer stared at me. Hard.

I tried to explain. "It's shorthand for privileged treatment in the canon —"

"Cannon? As in Revolutionary war?"

"No, C-A-N-O-N. A list of the texts which, over time, people have come to see as the most important."

"As in Shakespeare?"

"Yes, and Milton, Coleridge, Dickens, and so on. Primarily males — hence the phrase 'dead white men,' which is used to challenge the idea that only they had something significant to offer and that time was the

29

only way to measure worth."

The detective blinked rapidly. "Did you just say 'hence'?"

I nodded.

Archer sighed and tilted his head slightly. "Where is this list kept?"

"It isn't officially written down anywhere. But when you meet a colleague who subscribes to the *idea* of a fixed canon, you can tell."

"They want the list to stay the same?"

"Yes. Anything new is typically viewed as a threat."

"A threat?" He stiffened. "What do you mean?"

"Academics are deeply territorial. They want to preserve the importance of their topics."

"I see." His shoulders relaxed slightly. "But if it isn't written down, how does the list come into play?"

"Curriculum, for one thing. Authors included in programs, courses, and textbooks are presumably vital for students to know, while those excluded are not. It's also related to scholarship — it's generally much harder for professors to publish research on an author who is not already accepted as essential."

At Archer's puzzled expression, I tried to

streamline things: "It all comes down to who gets to determine the importance of texts, which has far-reaching consequences. It's about power, basically."

"Understood." He rubbed his forehead as if he had a headache.

I sat back, exhausted.

"So let's return to this afternoon. You went into the room and saw Dr. Higgins. Is there anything else you can tell me about the room itself?"

"I don't know. Everything sort of went into slow motion. Oh, Judith told me to call 911."

"What was Judith doing?"

"Just standing there, I think."

"How does Judith feel about Roland?"

I shrugged. "Not sure, really. I only met her a few weeks ago. She seems nice, though."

The detective looked grim. "Most people do. At first."

CHAPTER 3

A week later, the last vestiges of afternoon sun warmed the back of my black cotton dress as I walked slowly towards First Methodist church for Roland's memorial service. Although Colorado lacked the brutal humidity of my native New York, it was still plenty hot, even this late in the day. The front lawn of the church was filled with small groups of unfamiliar people murmuring to one another. I stepped over a flowerbed and edged onto the sidewalk uneasily.

"Lila!"

I heard Calista's voice from the main steps of the church, where she stood at the top, waving me over impatiently. Today she wore a simple black sheath, army boots, and a tiny hat with a small veil — appropriately somber fare yet still with her own special flair. Making my way through the crowd, I joined her.

She smiled. "Come sit with me. I haven't

seen Judith yet but she'll be here. How are you doing?"

"Overwhelmed. And already behind on my grading. Does the pace ever slow down?"

"Not really. It's a race until the semester's over. Are you feeling better about your conversation with the detective?" Her eyes caught on something behind me. "Speak of the devil. Don't look now."

I turned around to see Archer climbing the stairs. He gave me a brief nod.

"Hello —" said Calista, to his back as he disappeared into the church. "Well, he might be cute, but he isn't the friendliest person I've ever met. I met him at a charity event last year, and he spent the whole time sitting in a corner by himself."

"I think he's more the strong, silent type. And yes, I'm better now, thanks. It was just kind of intense."

Organ music began to play softly at that moment, so we went through the double doors and sat in a back row pew, watching the small church fill gradually with mourners in front of us. Most of the English faculty members were in attendance as well as a number of students. It was excessively warm in the room, despite the rotation of three oversized ceiling fans above, and many individuals fanned themselves with pro-

33

grams. I looked down at mine, which provided a list of prayers, hymns, and speakers, including Reverend Conrad Masters, Professor Spencer Bartholomew, and Professor Norton Smythe. Refreshments would follow in the reception room.

Across the aisle, Judith waved at us and slid into the row next to Detective Archer. They nodded at each other, then rose along with the rest of the congregation to sing the first hymn. Stained-glass windows on either side of the church glowed, and the light from outside cast ruby, gold, and indigo beams across the rows of people before us. Although I hadn't known Roland very well, the quiet splendor of that sight, along with the united voices of the people gathered here in his honor, moved me. I found myself having to wipe away a tear.

After the service, I followed Calista into the church's surprisingly spacious reception room, where we were offered paper cups of lukewarm coffee and butter cookies. A dark-suited Judith flung herself at us with arms outstretched and embraced us both. We chatted briefly about the service.

"How are things going with our project?" Judith asked Calista.

"Oh, right, I wanted to tell Lila." Calista

turned to me. "We offer a Gender Studies minor through the magic of cross-listed classes, and Judith and I are working on recruiting professors from various disciplines in order to grow into a major. We're always looking for people to join us."

"I'd love to, as soon as I get some momentum here and figure everything out."

"If you do, please let the rest of us in on it." She arched a well-groomed eyebrow. "Stonedale has its official procedures for paperwork to swim upward through the levels, but things tend to happen in mysterious and unofficial ways. I'm still trying to figure it out myself."

A tall gray-haired man in a black suit put an arm around Judith and thrust his head into the middle of the group. "Hello, everyone."

"Spence." Judith hugged her husband.

He kissed Calista on the cheek and gave me a firm handshake. "Lila, I'm sorry I wasn't able to greet you at the faculty meeting on Friday, due to . . . the incident." Spencer lowered his voice on the last part and shook his head sadly. "He will be missed."

"Your eulogy was very kind," I said. He had praised Higgins's "eminently dignified scholarship" and "sense of fraternal bond."

"We've all known Rolly for eons," said Judith. "In fact, he's the one who introduced me to Spence."

"And for that," Spencer smiled, "I am forever in his debt."

She touched his face gently. "You are sweet, my darling. Have you spoken to the family?"

"Not yet. His brother Eldon is the only remaining member." He pointed to a slightly younger-looking version of Roland — right down to the rimless glasses — standing in the corner beside a shiny silver coffee dispenser. A man strongly resembling Franklin Delano Roosevelt was talking earnestly to him.

Judith squinted and craned her neck forward slightly. "Is that Trawley accosting him?"

Spencer grimaced. "Yes. Probably suggesting that a generous donation would ensure the longevity of Rolly's legacy or some such."

"Is there any way we could save the poor man? It's hardly the right time."

"If he doesn't approach him here, it will just happen elsewhere, Jude. But I'll try to give Eldon a break — need to offer my own condolences, anyway. Speak to you later, all." He ambled over to the corner. I was

36

struck by how well-suited Spencer and Judith seemed to be.

"Who is Trawley?" I hadn't met him yet.

"Chancellor Trawley Wellington," Calista said. "Harvard man and don't you forget it —"

Judith coughed delicately. "Dear, perhaps we might hold off on the lengthy description for another time? The walls have ears, you know."

"Sorry, Judith." Calista looked chastened. "You're right. I should probably go home anyway."

Judith smiled at her, then patted my shoulder. "Perhaps you should aim for some quiet time tonight too. You've been through something quite out of the ordinary this week. But please do call me if you need anything."

I happened to agree with her suggestion and followed Calista straight for the exit after we'd bid Judith goodbye. We'd made it almost to the door when I heard someone call Calista's name.

Norton Smythe, his comb-over bobbing vigorously as he hurried towards us, waved his antique pipe of polished honey-colored wood curving gradually into a brown handle. He was a fiftyish medieval scholar who, like Spencer, had also spoken at the service, painting a glowing picture of Roland's qualities. His bronze medallion tie was askew, granting him a slightly unbalanced air.

I began to compliment him on his tribute to Roland, but he interrupted me.

"You shouldn't have murdered my friend." Norton's lips were pulled back into a snarl as he spat the words. He jabbed the pipe in Calista's direction. She began slowly edging backwards.

I stepped between them as he tilted forward, hitting me with a cloud of fetid breath.

"Stop right there." I raised my right hand, palm out in front of me like a cop directing traffic, and raised my voice, hoping to attract the attention of any nearby individual. Calista pushed the door open and went outside.

His features seemed to rearrange themselves into something malevolent and grotesque.

"I *know* you did it, Calista!" he called after her, clenching his empty hand into a fist.

"I don't know why you think that, but it's not true, Norton," I said.

"She did. I saw the knife in her office. And she'll pay for what she's done," he hissed, his face suddenly mere inches from mine.

I spun around, threw my body onto the

pressure bar of the door, and slipped through the opening. As I ran down the stairs into the cool twilight, I could hear him laughing.

Norton's aggressiveness had shaken us both. Neither one of us thought he had seemed drunk — just furious. Calista and I compared notes on his behavior as we walked the five blocks to Crescent Street. By the time we arrived at Calista's, I was feeling somewhat normal again.

Her house, like my own — just a few blocks away — was a single-floor bungalow, probably built in the 1920s, but hers was painted a rosy peach. The red shutters and white trim provided a lively contrast, as did the bright purple of her Russian Sage, which held their color even into the fall. I wanted to buy some for my own front garden straightaway.

"Come in and have some dinner, Lila. I could use the company."

"Sure," I said, following her up the stone steps.

The inside of her home was as cheery as the outside, with soft yellow walls and an assortment of art prints creating a warm and inviting space. She directed me to the purple sofa accented with batik pillows, disappeared through an archway to the kitchen, and called back over her shoulder. "Just have to get some food warmed up — leftovers, okay? — and pour some wine. Big glasses of wine, obviously."

"Obviously."

She returned with two full-to-the-brim goblets. Clearly, we weren't going to pretend to savor the bouquet; tonight, we were drinking for medicinal purposes. I welcomed anything that would help me relax. I still felt jittery from Norton's accusations.

We both took sips and settled back.

"What was Norton talking about? That was so weird," I asked.

A strange look crossed her face. She traced the rim of the wine glass with her finger.

"Cal, tell me. What's going on?"

"Nothing is going on," she said quickly. "But he wasn't lying — I did have a knife in my office. And it disappeared." She took a large drink of her wine.

"What do you mean you had a *knife* in your office? Who keeps a knife in their office? Why was it there?"

"It's . . . decorative." Calista set her glass carefully on the dark wood coffee table, then got up and began to pace back and forth across the kilim rug. "About a week ago,

40

Norton happened to stop by when the knife was on my desk. He didn't mention a thing about it then, but clearly he saw it because — well, you heard what he said." She whirled around to face me. "The thing is, someone stole it."

"Stole it?"

"Yes. And I'm worried it's the same knife that was used to kill Roland."

I stared at Calista.

She slid back onto the sofa, looking pale and defeated.

"It can't be the same knife. You said it was just for decoration."

"True," she said, "but it still had a blade."

"You weren't questioned by the police or anything?"

"Not yet," she said. "But my fingerprints are all over it. I don't know what to do, Lila. Should I call and tell them my knife is probably the one that killed Roland?"

"Well, not like that, exactly," I said. "Maybe just report that it's missing?"

"Of course. I don't know why I didn't think of that." She flashed me a grateful smile, and some color came back into her cheeks.

"They might still question you — especially if it is the murder weapon."

"I know," she said. "But I don't have

41

anything to hide."

"Are you sure the knife isn't just lost? When's the last time you saw it?"

"That day. And yes, I'm sure. I tore my office apart. Anyway, have I mentioned how glad I am that you're here? Thanks for the advice."

"Just doing my cousinly duty," I said, patting her arm.

"Speaking of, how's Aunt Vi?"

"Busy as ever."

"Seems like it, judging from her Twitter feed." Calista snapped her fingers. "And I almost forgot about feeding you, Lil. Let me bring out our dinner."

She bustled into the kitchen and I sank deeper into the cushions of the extraordinarily comfortable sofa. I'd probably fall asleep if I tried to grade on it.

A brown cat with huge yellow eyes sidled into the room. I held my hand out for her to sniff, which she did delicately. Calista had named her after the famous suffragist Elizabeth Cady Stanton because she was a fierce and scrappy kitten. It appeared she'd grown calmer since then — rather than boomeranging through the room swatting at anything that got in her way, as she used to do, Cady settled carefully on my feet and started purring.

My gaze landed on the framed photos on Calista's bookshelves, most of them pictures from our childhood. My mother and aunt were both artists, and we'd all lived in a small upstate New York town so they could collaborate on projects. I studied the familiar scenes, lingering on one I'd snapped of Mom, Aunt Rose, and Uncle Paul on the shore of Lake Ontario — the three of them arm in arm, squinting in the bright sun. I could practically hear the waves crashing behind them. It had been our last summer together; my aunt and uncle had been killed in a car accident when Calista was ten. My cousin had come to live with my mother and me — I had never known who my father was — from that day forward. Mom believed the best way to outpace the grief was to keep moving, so she applied for all kinds of art grants, fellowships, colonies, and various teaching positions. That created a whole different set of issues for Calista and me, though, like always being the new kids at yet another in a long blur of schools. Coming to Stonedale felt a little like that all over again.

My meandering thoughts were interrupted when Calista arrived, setting down a tray with utensils and two plates filled with red pepper quiche, sautéed ginger broccoli with almonds, and spinach salad with cranberries and feta cheese.

"My dining table is my desk, so we'll have to picnic here on the coffee table."

"Fine with me. This looks delicious, thank you."

We ate in companionable quiet for a few minutes.

I waved my fork over the table. "You know, your leftovers are fancier than my freshly baked — by which I mean heated in the microwave — dinners."

She laughed. "I do love to mess around in the kitchen. It satisfies some creative urge I can't get to through my poetry."

"Didn't you want to be a chef at one point?"

Calista grinned. "Yes. One of my many almost-careers, along with graphic design and public relations. Thank goodness I tried the MFA program — from day one, I knew I was in the right place."

"It must have been, because now you're up for tenure."

"Yes, which means I have to be careful." She sighed. "And Norton is already not a fan, if you know what I mean. He has made his disdain for me very clear."

"You mean, aside from what he did today?" I put my fork down and faced her.

"Yes. He's always making little negative comments here and there. Roland has done it too."

"Why?"

She nudged my shoulder with hers.

"Aw, you have so much to learn, sweetie. They don't *need* to have a reason."

"Could people like that prevent you from getting tenure?" I had heard that any grievance whatsoever — no matter how minor or unfairly held — could arise, phoenix-like, at any point, but I didn't understand how that translated into blocking a tenure bid.

"Technically yes," she said, settling back against the pillows and drawing up her knees. "Before the term started, I submitted a dossier documenting all the work I've done, which will be evaluated at multiple levels." She ticked them off on her fingers as she counted. "Department, chair, dean, college, provost, faculty senate, chancellor, board of trustees. And they all get a vote."

"I hadn't realized so many people were involved in the process."

"Yes, and because it's decided by votes, all someone has to do is cast enough doubt with whatever so-called evidence they think demonstrates my unworthiness and convince others to vote against me. And so far, it's not going well. The letter from the committee, which Norton chairs, supported me overall but did question the university press with which I published my first book because they've since gone under. The committee letter left the door open for Roland to make a bigger deal of that than it deserves. That's what the meeting was about the other day — he said he wanted clarification on a few things before finalizing his letter. But he also implied the letter was negative. Now it all depends on how the other levels interpret or agree with Roland's assessment. And so on."

"That sounds totally unfair."

"That would be it, you know. Once you are denied tenure, you're probably finished. Done. Goodbye, academia." She shrugged. "But it's out of my hands at this point."

I admired her calmness. "Would you have any method of protest after a decision is made?"

"You could always fight it. Hire a lawyer, bring a lawsuit against the school. Very expensive and, even if you won, which is rare, those battles tend to . . . taint things," she said slowly.

"You deserve tenure," I said firmly. "Presses go under all the time, and it doesn't reflect unfavorably on the author. Seems like a flimsy reason. I have to believe the other levels will dismiss that complaint."

"Maybe." She looked thoughtful. "Whatever the result, at least it will be over this spring."

Time to change the subject. "I just re-read your book before moving out here. How in the world did you produce an epic poem about the maiden/mother/crone archetype? It's amazing."

Calista brightened. "You are so kind — though extraordinarily biased."

"Your writing is incredible. I was thinking about assigning an excerpt in American Lit. Would you be willing to come in and talk to the students about it?"

"Absolutely. I'd be honored."

"Good, that's settled, then. The students will love it. What's the book you're working on now?"

"A collection of sestinas about the mythological goddesses."

"Aren't sestinas one of the hardest forms in which to write?"

She laughed. "That's why I chose them. I figured if I could do an entire book of sestinas, I'd never be afraid to launch a new collection again."

One thing I knew for sure: Calista wasn't the type to be afraid of anything.

CHAPTER 4

Monday morning, as I inserted my office key, the next door — with its poster of Nathaniel Hawthorne peering stiffly ahead as if his collar were too tight — swung open. I took in the faded polo shirt, cargo pants, longish brown hair, and bright blue eyes that brought to mind an eager puppy: Nate Clayton.

"When's your first class? Would you like to get a cup of coffee?" He smiled, his teeth white against his sunburned face, no doubt earned via a recent mountain climb or hike. "They brought a Starbucks to campus, praise be."

I consulted my watch. "My first class is in two hours."

"Perfect. Let's go to the union and, on the way, visit the fountain for good luck. It's a Stonedale tradition."

I pulled the door shut again, somewhat reluctantly, as I was inexplicably excited to spend time in my new office. But his enthusiasm was contagious, and I knew the office giddiness would wear off soon enough.

We headed out of Crandall Hall and kept to the outer perimeter sidewalk, passing Randsworth, the colossal building that housed the chancellor and other administrative VIPs. Crandall's columns, while moderately impressive, were nothing compared to the embellishments of Randsworth, which could have been a cathedral with its lavish turrets, spires, and other ornamentations. Presiding over campus directly across the circle from the entry gates, Randsworth announced its own importance.

I stopped and squinted. How interesting. Hadn't noticed before that it was topped with gargoyles.

"I know, right?" Nate said.

"What?"

"You said 'gargoyles.' "

"Out loud? That's embarrassing."

"I won't tell anyone. But you should know this campus is full of mysterious things. One of the gargoyles, it's said, changes expressions every ten years. And supposedly there are secret tunnels between certain buildings. And you know that statue of the woman holding the bird?"

"What statue?"

"It's halfway between Crandall and Randsworth — you can't see it now because it's around the corner and tucked under that big elm tree. Anyway, it simply appeared one day, and no one knows why or who she is."

"How wonderfully Gothic," I said.

"I knew we were on the same page the instant we met," he said. We turned onto one of the short walkways leading to the fountain embedded within the large circular expanse of well-manicured lawn at the center of campus. The achievement of healthy grass was no small feat given the dry Colorado climate, not to mention the thousands of shoes trodding on it regularly. "And here we are."

An immense sculpture of a man holding a book in one hand and a rifle in the other was surrounded by radiant arcs of splashing water. There were the usual coins on the bottom, despite the signs forbidding it. Nate plunged his hand into the clear water and invited me to do the same.

"So what are we doing here?"

I sat on the marble bench that ringed the pool.

"At the beginning of every term, we humbly request Jeremiah Randsworth's blessing so we might make it through the semester in one piece." He winked.

"Nice." I peered up at the statue. "Is that the man himself?"

"Yes, our illustrious university founder, circa 1850. Rugged settler and avid reader, as you can see from the not-so-subtle symbolism. Now, close your eyes and ask for protection. C'mon."

I submerged my hand.

"Try not to think of the many drunken fraternity pledges who have plunged naked into these same icy waters."

"Oh!" I hastily withdrew my hand.

He laughed. "Just kidding. Except not really because this fountain has seen its share of hazing, even though we at Stonedale are officially against it. As is every university."

"Of course."

He jumped up. "Let's get that coffee."

At a table in the corner of the student union with our steaming drinks before us, we compared educational backgrounds — he described the program at the University of Kansas, which he had enjoyed, and I recollected my years at NYU in kind.

"And now here we both are, out west to stake our proverbial claims." Nate blew on his coffee. "Don't you think it's somewhat shocking that we are the only Americanists here? I'm part one and you're part two. How well can the two of us really cover all of it?"

"I'm just grateful to have a job." That was the customary answer for any new hire, the correct response to practically any potentially political question.

"Right, right. I am too," he said quickly.

"Sorry," I said, meaning it. "That sounded a little prim, didn't it?"

"It's good practice for when we need to say it, though," said Nate, who suddenly resembled my idea of Huckleberry Finn: mischievous but compelling.

We smiled at each other.

"Have you met Simone Raleigh yet? She was also hired this year," Nate said.

"No. What's she like?"

Nate tilted his head and considered this. "Don't know yet. Seems smart."

"Okay." I should make an effort to find her. Perhaps she was feeling some of the same anxieties about being the new kid on the block — we could commiserate.

"Have you met everyone else? I assume you have studied the professor list on the faculty website in order to hit the ground running."

I laughed. "In fact I have."

"Excellent. All wise newbies do their research. And make no mistake, people do note whether or not you've done your homework around here." He produced a meaningful look.

"Good tip," I said.

He fixed his blue eyes on mine. "I heard you found Roland. How are you holding up?"

I shrugged.

Nate reached around the table and touched my arm lightly. "I can't imagine how awful this has been for you. It's hard enough to be the new person. If you want to talk about it, I'm here."

"Thanks." I glanced around the room packed with chattering students. It was hard to believe that just a few days ago I'd come into such close contact with death on this very campus. The students, with their colorful t-shirts and backpacks, were so vibrantly alive. "Maybe another time."

He looked out of the window next to us, focused on something in the distance. "Did I hear correctly that Calista is your cousin?"

"Yes."

"Are you close?"

"We grew up together."

"Cool," he said.

"She's the one who told me about the

opening and encouraged me to apply. I never thought I'd get the job, though. You know what the market is like."

He nodded. "I think there were around four hundred candidates for your position."

"I had no idea. Now it seems even more like a miracle." All the more reason not to mess this opportunity up.

"Has Calista heard anything from the tenure committee yet?"

"I think she received a letter, but I don't really know the details," I said. It was her news to tell, in any case.

"I hope she has a better experience than Tad Ruthersford. Did you hear about that?"

I shook my head. Tad was my next-door neighbor, but we hadn't talked much.

Nate leaned forward and lowered his voice. "I've never seen anything like it. We've all heard horrendous stories about going up for tenure, right? So-and-so hasn't published enough, or hasn't done enough service, or has angered the old guard and is therefore punished. And it's usually clear beforehand that there might be problems. But here's the thing: until Tad went up for tenure, Roland was always singing his praises, applauding Tad for the astuteness of his scholarship. But then Roland started making increasingly derisive comments about Tad's work. I don't know why."

"That sounds like a nightmare. Did he get tenure?"

"Yeah, but he had a rough time of it. He's been keeping a low profile ever since."

"Poor Tad."

"He's a good guy."

I felt slightly ill just thinking about the fact that eventually I'd have to put myself on the proverbial chopping block. Especially since tenure-track candidates needed to master the art of appearing to be compliant, which would require some major effort on my part.

"Just imagining it makes me queasy," he said, as if reading my thoughts.

"When do you go up?"

"The year before you do."

I was surprised. "You came to Stonedale last fall?"

"Yep," he said, smiling.

"But you seem so settled." It was even more than that: an air of ease not typical of most "junior faculty," a term that in and of itself displayed the academic power structure. It was a wonder they didn't make us wear beanies with little helicopter spinners on top until we were granted tenure.

"Well," he said, "next year at this time,

you'll feel as though you've been here for eons."

"In a good way?"

"Mostly," he said. "A few things aside."

"What do you mean?"

"There's a lot of pressure to publish quickly," he said. "I'd argue the expectation's not realistic. Finding time to write is a struggle since teaching, advising, and serving on committees is already a tremendous amount of work. To publish well, we need time to write well." He shrugged. "But no one's asking me."

After completing my dissertation last spring, I'd needed a break from the deeply exhausting zone of intensity required to produce a lengthy piece of scholarly writing, but clearly I would need to get back to it. "What are you working on?"

"I'm finishing up a book manuscript to send out this winter. Fingers crossed."

"That's exciting. What's your topic?"

"Hawthorne. Specifically, *The Blithedale Romance*. I wrote about several of his novels in my dissertation, but I've since limited my focus. Managed to place one of the other chapters in a respectable journal and expanded the one on *Blithedale* into a book."

"I adore *Blithedale*. Absolutely love it."

"It's great, isn't it? Mesmerism, obsession,

and secret love. It's been snubbed, I think, aside from the perfunctory acknowledgment given all so-called 'lesser works' of an acclaimed author. *Seven Gables* and *Scarlet Letter* are powerful, of course, but *Blithedale* is nothing to sneeze at, as it manages to pull off some remarkable feats of its own. At least that's the thrust of my argument, played out over three hundred pages and couched in terminology far more impressive and sophisticated than that."

"Sounds fascinating. I'd love to read it."

"You may be the only one who ever does." We sipped our coffee in amiable silence. Glancing at my watch, I realized I only had twenty minutes before class started and gasped.

Nate caught my eye. "Time to go? Where's your class?"

"Crandall."

"Our very own stomping grounds. Shall we head back?"

When I was an adjunct, it seemed as though the classes were always scheduled at the opposite side of campus, and I'd become used to panicked cross-campus jogs. To be in the same building as my office? Heavenly. Thus, it was with a sense of minor jubilation that I accompanied Nate across the green.

CHAPTER 5

On Wednesday, I was climbing the marble stairs to the English department when Judith burst around the corner, caught sight of me, and fluttered her fingers. "Lila, I've just been to your office. We have a mentoring meeting this afternoon — there was a note in my box, but I just found it buried among a summer's worth of mail. With everything that's happened, I haven't had a chance to go through it all until this morning. Are you free, dear? We only have five minutes to fly over to Randsworth Hall, if so."

"I'm supposed to have office hours —"

"You can cancel them for these," Judith interjected. "I've already informed Millicent for you. She'll put a note on your door to let students know."

I'd hoped to use my office hours to do some reading for class, but I guess that would have to wait. There never seemed to be enough time in the day to catch up. I tried to arrange my face into what I hoped was an eager expression.

As we hurried across the green, chatting about our classes, I caught sight of the stone gargoyles looming from the roof of Randsworth and felt a sudden chill. Although frightening away evil spirits was said to be one of their purposes, I had the impression the gray statues were sending something malicious towards us instead. I shook my head to clear the fanciful thoughts, and soon we had reached a seminar room on the second floor of Randsworth, where approximately twenty people sat around a collection of tables arranged in a U-shape. Judith and I claimed the last two seats with relief.

During the introductions, I noticed a woman with a long blonde French braid tapping furiously on her cell phone. She wore a red fitted jacket with a black collar, which created a highly equestrian effect. I wondered if she planned to go riding — or even on a hunt — after this meeting. It wasn't out of the question, given we were in Stonedale. She texted right up until it was her turn to speak, then gracefully slipped the phone onto the table.

"Simone Raleigh," she said. "English."

Ah, the elusive fellow newbie. I had been looking forward to meeting her.

A few hours later, we had been thoroughly welcomed by Dean Okoye, a jovial spokesperson for the university's many virtues. Chancellor Wellington had also made a lengthy plea for our efforts to uphold the "golden reputation of our beloved school" through our future achievements and invited us to contribute generously to the annual giving fund. All new professors had introduced ourselves and agreed to read through the faculty handbook — an epic tome certain to require many hours of deciphering small print — before the next mentoring meeting.

Judith turned to me when we'd run out of speakers. "That's all for now, it appears. Would you like a lift home?"

"I would love a ride, thanks."

Simone strode up and hugged Judith.

"Let me introduce you two before I have a quick word with the chancellor." Judith repeated our names and left us facing one another.

"Hello," I said to Simone, smiling. "Happy to meet you."

She smoothed her shining hair back, an astonishingly large diamond on her engagement finger catching the light. "What department are you in again?" she inquired, her lips curved into a semblance of a smile, the kind plastered on as social nicety to cover sheer indifference.

"English. With you."

"Really?" She sounded surprised, as if we all hadn't just introduced ourselves in the meeting. She must not have been listening. "What's your area?"

"American."

She scowled. It seemed an odd reaction. Did she not like American literature?

"Oh," she said. After a prolonged silence, it was clear she had nothing else to add.

"What's yours?"

"Victorian literature, with a specialty in Charlotte Brontë."

"I love *Jane Eyre.*"

"Everybody does," she said, with a hint of exasperation.

I pretended not to notice. "What are you teaching this semester?"

As she reeled off her courses, I listened carefully and made politely approving sounds when it seemed expected. I didn't quite know what to make of Dr. Raleigh. She reminded me of a particularly self-satisfied cat I'd once known.

Judith reappeared in a cloud of lavender

scent. "Shall we go?"

Gratefully, I accepted. We were making our way out of the meeting room when I felt a heavy hand on my shoulder.

"Dr. Maclean, may I borrow you?" I recognized the well-modulated tones of Chancellor Wellington.

"I'll meet you downstairs," said Judith.

The chancellor bared his teeth in what I'm sure he imagined was a kindly smile but which came off more like a wolf staring at his supper.

"How may I help you?" I asked.

"Judith and I have already spoken about this matter, but I wanted to have a chat with you as well." He paused for a long while, during which I tried to stand up a little straighter. "You're one of the people who found Dr. Higgins, yes?"

"Yes," I said.

"Must have been quite a shock. How are you handling it?"

"I'm . . . managing, thank you."

He leaned against the wall next to the door and sniffed, clearly waiting for me to say something else. I wasn't sure what else there was to say, so I remained silent, readjusting the heavy satchel strap digging into my shoulder.

"Not good for the university, a murder.

Not good at all," he said.

My mouth fell open. I snapped it shut.

"We like our professors to keep a certain distance from unsavory events. I strongly suggest you try to avoid such unpleasantness in the future." He watched my face closely.

"Understood," I said.

"There's not anything you need to tell me, is there, Dr. Maclean?"

"About?" I seemed unable to form complete sentences.

"About your involvement in Dr. Higgins's . . . ah . . . demise." He looked away, as if to give me some privacy to work up a suitable confession.

"No, sir."

After an extended pause, he nodded and marched through the doorway.

I stumbled downstairs and was whisked in the luxurious comfort of Judith's BMW to my doorstep. During the drive, she tried to alleviate my distress about the encounter I'd had with the chancellor.

"He pretty much asked me outright if I'd killed Roland," I said. "Did he ask you that?"

She smiled. "No, dear. But he's known me forever."

"So because I just got here, I'm the most

likely murderer? Is that what everyone thinks?"

"Some may think so, Lila." At least she was honest. "People are looking for quick answers. They're scared."

"Well, in that case, at least I'm not the only one being accused," I said.

"What do you mean?"

I described Norton's accusations about Calista and was gratified that Judith seemed almost as shocked as I had been.

"How upsetting," she said, as we made a right onto Haven Street. "Norton was probably displacing his grief on her. And the chancellor, well, he does have to think about the school's reputation, though he was clumsy with you, to be sure. It's unfair, but sentiments are always heightened in such situations."

"In both cases, it seemed more hostile than sad."

"Emotions don't always translate clearly, dear. Not that I condone either one's behaviors. I'm sorry Norton was so beastly. And I'm sorry the chancellor implied distrust of you. But please try not to think the worst of us here at Stonedale. You must remember that people don't know you very well yet."

"True. But I don't think being new should

be treated like some kind of crime," I said, a bit more huffily than I meant to.

"You're absolutely right," she said, in a soothing tone. "I'm sorry you've been caught up in this whole situation. If it makes you feel any better, I don't think you killed Roland."

What a surreal conversation.

"Thanks, Judith. I appreciate that. Do you have any idea who might have done it?"

She looked out the windshield. "I've been thinking about that quite a bit, dear. I wish I did."

"There haven't been any particularly nasty political fights involving Roland?"

"Oh, I wouldn't say *that*," Judith said, laughing. "There have been plenty — far more than I can count over the years, in fact. But none of them stands out."

I nodded, then opened the door to climb out, wondering if she knew more than she was saying and, if so, why she wouldn't want to share it with me.

After I waved goodbye to Judith, I turned to proceed up the short walkway to my house. I paused at the sight of someone sitting on my front steps. The evening shadows made it difficult to make out the person's features.

"Hello?" I called.

"It's me, Tad." My neighbor slid forward with a graceful movement. The sudden spill of illumination across his face from a nearby street light accentuated his agreeable smile. "Where've you been?"

"Mentoring meeting."

"Oh, how dreadful." Tad and I had spoken a few times in the department once we'd discovered that we lived next door to each other, but not at any great length. I didn't know much about him, other than that he taught early British Lit and had trouble with tenure last year, as Nate had mentioned. "Do you have time for a drink?"

I hesitated, torn between collegial curiosity and a strong desire to go inside and put my feet up. "I should really do some class prep . . ."

Tad smiled. "How about a very small and very quick one?"

Curiosity won. "Okay."

"Right this way." I followed him across the yard, through the front door, and into a sitting room on the left. It was furnished attractively in a Ralph Lauren sort of way, with a leather sofa and club chairs flanking an obviously expensive but slightly worn rug in front of a fireplace. "Be right back," he said over his shoulder as he headed to the kitchen.

I crossed the room to inspect a black frame hung above the fireplace, inside of which was a quotation rendered with elegant decorative script on cream parchment.

"I saw the Cloud, tho' I did not foresee the Storm."

Tad reappeared and handed me a glass of red wine. "Ah, you found my person. The writer with whom I spent all of my dissertation-writing years and every manuscript-writing moment since. He comforts me." He shrugged sheepishly.

I smiled. " 'I am giving an account of what was, not of what ought or ought not to be.' "

He laughed. "You've read *Moll Flanders.* You never know these days what's covered at a given school. I am undoubtedly biased, but I think Daniel Defoe should be part of everyone's curriculum — nay, he should be part of everyone's décor!"

Now it was my turn to laugh. "I understand completely. When I was writing my dissertation, I plastered my walls with quotations from Isabella Dare."

"Have you published on her?" He seemed genuinely interested.

"Not yet."

"Well, I look forward to reading your words about her in the future." He stepped close to the dark brown sofa. "Shall we make ourselves comfortable?"

I settled into the buttery soft leather and tasted the wine, a black cherry cabernet with a hint of vanilla. "This is exquisite."

"My family's label. I'm glad you like it." Tad gave me a stunning smile as I tried to appear nonchalant about the fact that his family owned a vineyard or two. "In retrospect, I would have been better off framing Alexander Pope's 'Blessed is he who expects nothing, for he shall never be disappointed.' It would have prepared me more for the experience with Roland. Shall I tell you the tale? You'll hear about it sooner or later, and you might as well hear it directly from me."

I took another sip of the velvety wine and felt my shoulders relax ever so slightly. "Please."

His brown eyes seemed to darken — or was it a trick of the light? "To put it simply, he tried to kill me."

CHAPTER 6

"*Kill* you?"

Tad laughed bitterly. "Yes. That bastard did everything in his power to prevent me from getting tenure. Which would have slaughtered my career, as he bloody well knew."

"What happened?"

"He told the committee the newer journals I'd published in weren't of sufficient status and argued that those publications shouldn't count." He gripped his wine glass tightly. "If that weren't enough, he circulated an email to the department, chastising us all for not setting our sights high enough, encouraging us to send our work to, and I quote, 'the *only* acceptable journals, those with longstanding reputations.' Roland never mentioned my name, but everyone knew whom he meant. I had to request additional letters of support from" — he used air quotes — "recognized scholars in the field."

We shared a commiserative look. "I'm so sorry, Tad. How awful."

He took a long drink before continuing. "It was. I'd left myself vulnerable by submitting a group of critical articles instead of a book-length study. Roland had told me when I was hired that either was acceptable, but it turns out that equivalence wasn't written down anywhere. He fought as hard as he could to get rid of me. I fought as hard as I could to stay."

"That doesn't seem right." Roland's warning about junior faculty needing to be quiet came back to me. I'd thought it was directed at me, but perhaps he felt that way about everyone.

"No, it doesn't. And when I was tenured, it didn't feel appropriately victorious, especially since I suspect it took a call from Tad Senior."

"Your father was involved?"

"He was the one who hired Roland back in the days of yore. And of course the chancellor saw the error of Roland's ways after a gentle reminder of Father's legacy, by which I mean enduring financial generosity." He raised his glass. "A toast to family."

I didn't know what to say about that, so I

opted for the logical question. "Why do you think Roland turned against you?"

Tad snorted. "I disagreed with him a few times on curricular matters. Maybe that was enough. Or perhaps it had to do with him having read what I actually wrote, rather than just patting me on the head for what he thought I wrote. In which case I was just the latest in a long line of efforts to keep the academy pure. He had appointed himself gatekeeper."

"Gatekeeper?"

"Yes, Roland felt the application of contemporary critical theory to literature was a destructive force — 'a muddying flood,' he called it — and viewed anyone who had the audacity to wield theory as a threat to his beloved tradition. But that was just *one* of his projects — he also objected to any attention paid to newly discovered writers, especially those of the 'fairer sex,' as he liked to say."

I nodded. "I sensed that, actually."

"Oh right, he protested about your research too."

"He did?" I was suddenly short of breath. Although Roland had asked challenging questions after the presentation I'd given during my campus interview, I had figured it was intentionally done to see how the candidate holds up under pressure and all that. It's a component of the culture: the dissertation defense provides another case in point. Anyone who has presented at an academic conference has likely also encountered the trend for complicated — sometimes completely inscrutable — interrogations by scholarly audience members. And there are many reasons, aside from wanting a genuine answer, that such questions are asked. One never knows if the questioner is probing the depth of the speaker's knowledge, foregrounding their own area of expertise, or just being ornery.

"Yes, he stood up in the faculty meeting and argued we should hire the other candidate, a woman from Notre Dame who had demonstrated what Roland perceived as the 'good sense' to write a dissertation comparing Robert Frost to John Donne."

I tried to process the fact that there had been controversy about my hiring.

Tad paused.

"I shouldn't have mentioned that."

"Please, go on."

"No one agreed with him. The rest of us wanted to hire you, but he tried several times to convince us your research was necessarily more limited because your work on Isabella Dare was . . ." He seemed uncomfortable.

I waited. The tick of the ebony mantel clock was deafening.

"Tad, please go on. I would prefer to know. I can handle it, promise."

"I'm trying to remember exactly what he said." Tad studied the ceiling. "Oh yes — your topic was 'not important enough to guarantee publication, much less acclaim for our esteemed reputation.' He also tried to claim that your presentation seemed 'aggressively feminist.' "

"Wow." I froze, my face flaming and my ears ringing. "Unimportant *and* aggressive?"

He caught sight of my expression and looked apologetic. "Lila, don't take it personally. No one listened, I swear — we were all so used to him attacking something or other for no reason. He was a bit of a joke and only had a few friends in the department. Any respect he once commanded dissipated once we all discovered what a horrible person he was."

I took a deep breath and let it out slowly. "Did you ever speak with him after the tenure issue?"

"Not until this fall. We went on summer break after the announcement, and I retired to my family's place in the Hamptons as soon as possible."

"Well, I hope that was restorative." The Hamptons sounded about right, considering the Ruthersfords' ability to have their very own family vineyards.

"It was indeed. I returned ready to put my feelings about Roland Higgins behind me, though obviously it takes time. I'm working on it. But enough about *that* sordid business. Let's move on to more current sordidness — have you recovered from finding his body?" I flinched. Putting it that way seemed so harsh. I'd spent a number of sleepless nights reliving, in nauseating, slow-motion detail, the moment I'd realized what I was seeing on the table. It took pronounced effort to squash that horror. "Oh, I'm sorry," Tad said, in a softer voice. "Not ready to talk about it?"

"No. It was too terrible. I'm sorry."

"Fair enough. How was the service?"

"It was dignified."

Tad's lip curled. "Of course. Putting the best face forward — quintessential Stonedale. Who from the department spoke?"

"Spencer and Norton. They truly seemed to care about him."

"They'd been colleagues long enough to forgive him his sins." While I was trying to decide whether or not to bring up Norton's wild accusation, the mantel clock chimed. Tad took my wine glass gently from my hand and set it on the table. "But we can talk more later — I believe you said you had professorial duties to attend to this evening?"

"Thanks. And it's been lovely talking with you. I was hoping we'd have a chance."

"Sorry it took me so long to act civilized." He rubbed his face briskly. "It's still rather embarrassing, having to walk into that department after last year. I've been hiding."

"Why is it embarrassing? You have tenure."

"I grew up in Stonedale. Literally on campus — hell, in our department, even. Everyone knew what was going on. Not to mention my father has since taken every opportunity to remind me what a failure I am. When he was a professor here, he was a star. Sailed right through the tenure process with nary a glitch."

"But surely he knows that academic politics play a role —"

"Yes, but he thinks that's my fault too. Says he raised me to be able to navigate them better," said Tad glumly.

"I'm sorry," I said. "Do your parents still live in Stonedale?"

"They alternate between Aspen in the winter and the Hamptons in the summer. They also have a house down here for the other seasons. But I see them all the time. Command performances at the Ruthersford manse. You know how it is."

Not really.

Later that evening, I was curled up on my sofa, holding a mug of herbal tea with one hand and pulling at a loose thread on my favorite black yoga pants — someday I was actually going to have to take up yoga if I kept wearing them — with the other. I thought about what Tad had been through. A lesser person might have walked away from Stonedale altogether. I hoped over time he would be able to enjoy, even celebrate, the fact that he'd made it through the gauntlet.

I set my tea on the plastic crate currently in use as an end table and looked around the room. My furnishings were coming together slowly, thanks to Craigslist, but I still had some gaps to fill. So far, I'd scored the soft red chenille sofa in perfect condition, a brown oak dining table set with only one wobbly chair, and a matching coffee table with a small corner scratch that didn't bother me a bit. It was a good thing I wasn't picky about décor, because I couldn't afford much. Some people think all professors make a lot of money, which is not the case across the board. Not to mention many of us will be paying off school loans for decades to come. Although choosing a career in higher education doesn't always make financial sense, I was grateful for the opportunity to teach.

I stared at the textbooks for my current courses — American Literature since 1865 and Gothic Literature — and tried to choose which one to prepare first. As I reached for the pile of books on the coffee table, my cell phone rang, the screen displaying Calista's name. Saved by the bell. We spent a few minutes talking about classes, then I steered the conversation to Tad.

"Hey, what's your take on Tad's tenure fight? He just told me about it."

"That's good, I suppose, that he can talk about it. Unless he's being obsessive and harping on it. It's one of those things that would probably be better left behind him."

"Is it true Roland went out of his way to blackball Tad?"

"And Spencer got all caught up in it as well," Calista said.

"Judith's husband?" That was news.

"How?"

"Spencer and Roland were close friends but super competitive with one another. It didn't help that they were both Renaissance scholars, though Spencer worked on Christopher Marlowe and Roland was a Shakespearean. Spencer's work is very interesting — he has done fresh things with *Doctor Faustus*. But the way Roland wrote about women characters was disgusting. He makes all these claims about how their bodies corrupt the moral landscape. Ick."

I made a mental note to search for some of Roland's scholarship. "How did Spencer get involved, then?"

"Well, after Roland put out that email about prestigious journals, it was obvious he was trying to make Tad look bad. I should say Tad was a trouper about it, overall. He never bad-mouthed anyone: he just started showing up pale and disheveled, as if he weren't sleeping or taking care of himself. We all tried to comfort him, but that didn't accomplish much . . ."

"Spencer?" I reminded her.

She made a sound of exasperation. "That's where I was headed. So at the last spring faculty meeting, Spencer stood up and thanked us for our hard work over the year, then added that he did not want any of us to think Roland's email had been meant to speak for the feelings of all senior faculty. We should be proud, he said, of our publications in academic journals both old and new. The room burst out in applause and Roland's face went dark purple as he sat there, sputtering."

"Wow."

"It was awesome. And a few days later, Tad's tenure was officially announced and we all went home for summer. But rumor had it Spencer and Roland stopped speaking to each other after that meeting."

Curiouser and curiouser. "Any idea why Spencer might have done that?"

"No. He always seemed to have Roland's back. I mean, he didn't always agree with him, but when they did have a public confrontation of ideas, he made sure Roland was treated with respect and that he had a graceful exit opportunity available."

I had met others who acted like Roland — overinflated egos are easy to find in academia — and they usually did reserve one corner for allies. They might be terribly condescending to students but not to colleagues. Or they were rude to most people but had a few select friends to whom they chortled about the supposed inferiority of everyone else.

Roland seemed to have alienated almost everyone who knew him, judging from the anecdotes piling up — but not, it appeared, Spencer. At least until the Tad situation. I filed that away for future contemplation.

"The tributes to Roland at the memorial service made him sound practically saintly."

"Well, Stonedale has a reputation to maintain, first and foremost. We may fight like cats and dogs within our own walls, but we don't let the villagers see. Wasn't that on page one of your faculty handbook?" She chuckled.

"You're funny."

"I'm surprised Addison Goldman didn't speak. They were extremely close friends, though I personally think Roland treated Addison awfully — almost like an indentured servant."

"What about Judith? Was he respectful of her?"

"Well, I know Roland introduced Judith to Spencer. For a while, they were all good friends with another woman too — whose position you took, actually — Elisabetta Vega. But after Spencer and Judith's wedding, Roland started hanging around with Addison instead. Third-wheel syndrome, I guess."

"Hmm."

Calista continued, "It's sad to admit, but Roland was almost universally loathed. Though in our defense, he was so mean it was impossible to like him."

"No redeeming qualities whatsoever?"

The line was quiet while she thought.

"He did wear some interesting ties."

CHAPTER 7

As I packed my satchel Friday morning, Tad's description of the hiring process flashed through my mind. Was Roland the only one who hadn't wanted me at Stonedale, or was Tad just trying to spare my feelings? The tiny snippet he shared about the departmental discussion of my scholarship was upsetting enough — and who knows what else was said? I yanked the flap over the bag with perhaps more force than was necessary and snapped the nickel clips shut.

The indignation subsided during a breezy walk to campus, and by the time I reached my office, I was determined to introduce positive energy into my life by organizing all teaching documents into easy-to-locate folders. Several hours of applying order to my small corner of Crandall Hall was invigorating. When it was time for the faculty meeting, I pushed the file cabinet closed with a sense of satisfaction.

We gathered in the freshly painted and re-carpeted department library, now re-assembled with different furniture: cherry bookcases lined the walls and a gleaming table dominated the center of the room. The black leather chairs were comfortable, if somewhat scuffed, though I knew that to be from use rather than the intentional marks sometimes given to pieces to achieve a "shabby chic" appearance. In this community, authentic distress is acceptable; faux distress is not. These chairs were cast-offs from the dean's office conference room, Calista had informed me, whispering, "Whatever was in here when Roland died was *destroyed.*" And thank goodness for that. Plus, it gave the dean a chance to upgrade his own furniture. A win-win.

Not counting Roland, of course. I winced at the thought.

Spencer, whom the dean had appointed interim chair, began the meeting by intro-ducing Simone and me as the newest mem-bers of the department, which resulted in a light smattering of applause. I wasn't ex-pecting that and was mortified to find myself smiling at the floor instead of at my colleagues. My reactions to any sort of public attention make no sense to anyone, not even me.

"Now," Spencer said, shifting tones, "I know we are all profoundly saddened by the loss of our longtime colleague. Let us have a moment of silence for Roland, who was deeply devoted to the work of our discipline." We bowed our heads until he began speaking again. "Thank you to all who attended the memorial service. His brother was most grateful to see Roland was a part of such a caring community. Finally, please continue to cooperate with the investigation — I know we are all committed to finding out what happened to our friend."

Addison, who taught Myth and Folklore, straightened his yellow bowtie, then lifted his hand tentatively, almost as if he wasn't fully committed to raising it. "I was wondering if we might discuss putting together a scholarship in Roland's name. He was such an important part of the department for so long . . ."

A ripple of responses around the conference table followed. Calista and Judith looked at each other, Tad tightened his lips, Nate gave him an encouraging smile. Clearly, Tad still had an emotional response to even the mention of Roland's name. Could he have killed Roland as payback? I chided myself for the dark thought — Tad had been so pleasant to me — but I didn't know anyone else who had a specific motive.

"Addison, perhaps you could write something up and discuss it with the scholarship committee? We would have to locate funding, but you're right that it would honor his dedication in a suitable fashion." Spencer turned to Judith. "Perhaps as chair of the committee, you could report back to the department at our next meeting?"

Judith agreed. She was wearing a stunning necklace today — a large stone pendant — with her olive jacket. Very stylish. Calista sat on her left, clad in an indigo wrap dress, staring attentively at Judith.

Wrenching my attention back to the meeting, I heard Willa Hartwell say something about a university-wide assessment project planned by the dean. As was fitting for her drama specialty, she underscored the need for our participation with exaggerated gesticulations that set her long hammered-silver earrings rocking. It was almost mesmerizing.

Willa concluded her plea with a request for volunteers to lead the charge. Unsurprisingly, no one spoke. Norton, his serene demeanor today in direct opposition to the menacing performance from the other night, finally held up and wiggled his pipe.

"I'll leave this in your capable hands then," she said to him. "We need two additional department representatives to report to Dean Okoye next week."

Norton warned us that he'd be knocking on office doors. I sincerely hoped I wasn't there when he knocked on mine.

Near the end of the meeting, Judith raised her hand. "As most of you know, Spencer and I host a gathering every year at our house during fall term. This year, in light of recent events, it seems especially important for us to come together. But I wanted to ask if you felt it would be appropriate. What do you think?" After a brief pause, heads around the table began to nod. "Good. Please try to join us: eight o'clock Sunday, 410 Fox Hollow Drive."

I crested the circular driveway in front of Judith's house — which was massive enough to warrant the title "mansion" — and handed over the keys for my twelve-year-old Honda Accord to a young man in a red vest. Probably a student hired for the event, he was polite and refrained from commenting on the state of my ancient ride. I smoothed my wine-colored secondhand Eileen Fisher jacket, hoping I was channeling appropriate professor-at-fancy-party vibes, and climbed the stone stairs into an entrance hall that was larger than my entire rented bungalow. People from the department were congregated before a long, curving stairway with wrought-iron banisters; a hallway on the right led to the kitchen, presumably, since a server with a tray pushed on a swinging door with her back and disappeared inside. I headed into the spacious, well-appointed room to the left. Millicent was bristling with her usual frostiness on one of the velvet couches, so I aimed instead for the wing chairs facing the fireplace. Tad was sitting in one of them, staring morosely into the fire.

"Enjoying the party, Tad?"

He adjusted the tasteful paisley tie he wore with his double-breasted blue suit. "Trying. And how are you this fine evening? Sorry I talked your ear off the other night."

I felt a surge of sympathy for him.

"Please don't apologize. It was illuminating, though I'm sorry you had to go through it."

"Thanks for your understanding." His face relaxed perceptibly. "Now on to a more exciting topic: did you bring a date tonight?"

"No." I couldn't even remember the last time I'd been on a proper date. How depressing. "Did you?"

Tad sighed. "I'm currently between boy-friends. Alas."

"Me too," I said, smiling at him.

"Well, we can keep each other company. I was just about to fetch myself another drink. Would you like one?"

I requested red wine and took his place in the extremely comfortable velvet chair. As I sat relaxing before the fire, I could hear snippets of conversation behind me surface from among the general buzzing.

". . . why do students think attendance on the first day of class doesn't count . . ."

". . . the classroom was so small, we were practically sitting on each other's laps . . ."

". . . then he said, 'Why can't you just add one more person to the roster? I am *paying* for this education, after all' . . ."

"Mind if I join you?" Calista, evoking Audrey Hepburn in a little black dress accessorized with long white gloves, slid into the vacant seat next to me. "What a cozy place to hide."

"I'm not hiding. I'm easing in gently."

"Well, I'm hiding. Millicent gave me the dirtiest look the instant I arrived. Cross-listing courses increases her workload, and she blames me for it."

"That's too bad."

"I don't know what to say, other than, hello, we're trying to fight the good fight here. If the university would just approve a Gender Studies department, I could hire someone else to take care of it."

"Do you think that will happen?"

"Eventually." She made a fist and shook it at the ceiling in the manner of Scarlett O'Hara. "As the Goddess is my witness."

Willa sailed up, layered in various shades of purple, with a scarf over a vest over a tunic over a skirt over stockings.

Calista squealed, jumping up to hug her. "I didn't know you were coming tonight."

"Wouldn't miss it," Willa said, in her melodious English accent.

Tad reappeared, holding two glasses of wine, one of which he handed to me. "Here you go, Lila. Calista, Willa, are you in need of libation?" Willa shook her head and Calista held up her own glass in response.

"Lila Maclean." I recognized Simone Raleigh's cultured purr behind me. She wore a slim pink sheath with a single strand of pearls, her blonde hair in a chignon — very Rich-Girl Barbie. "Would you be so kind as to introduce me?" She phrased it as if I'd forgotten my manners, the very moment before I had intended to display them. I went around the circle, identifying our colleagues, some of whom she had already met, but who was I to remind her of that? She gave a charming little wave. "Hello. I'm Simone."

"Our new Victorianist," said Tad, looking interested.

"Yes," she said, giving him a dazzling smile.

"Tad Ruthersford, Early British," he said, grinning broadly. "And where did you come from?"

She opened her flawlessly lipsticked mouth. "Harvard. The chancellor is a close friend of my mother's, who also went to Harvard *and* used to teach here at Stonedale. He urged me to apply when the opportunity arose, and" — her slim hand performed an elegant flourish — "voilà!"

A chorus of welcomes erupted. By the way everyone was beaming at her, it appeared they were already smitten.

"Did you and Lila know each other before?" Tad asked.

"We met at the mentoring meeting," said Simone, regarding me as if we were long-lost friends. She punctuated this by resting an arm around my shoulder. Since the situation called for it, I mustered up a smile, but I was baffled. Simone seemed to have undergone a personality transplant since the last time we spoke.

Willa turned to me. "Calista tells me you wrote a dissertation on an American author named Isabella Dare — what sorts of things did she write? I confess that I'm not familiar with her work. I'm sorry to have missed your interview presentation, by the way — I was giving a paper in London that week."

"She's a mystery writer, published in the 1970s, but it was a small press run, and she seems to have escaped scholarly notice. I have not found any articles or books on her at all. In fact, I had to backtrack through her publisher just to find biographical information beyond what was included with her books in the Library of Congress. Luckily, her publisher still had a file on her somewhere deep in their archives, so that was a good starting point."

"How did you come across her work?" Willa cocked her head inquisitively.

"I was at a used bookstore in New York City, searching for some out-of-print thing — I forget what now — and I came across a dusty box in the back of the store. The bookstore owner said the box had just come in from an estate sale, and she hadn't had a chance to shelve anything yet. She told me I could check inside if I wanted. There I found all three of Dare's books in perfect condition."

Willa shook her head sadly. "One wonders how many other works by unknown sisters are languishing in boxes around the world. I'm glad your director saw fit to approve the topic."

"So intriguing. How did you convince your committee to allow you to write on her?" Tad asked.

"She's a compelling storyteller, first of all. Think Agatha Christie meets Shirley Jackson, with a twist. My director Avery felt that claiming a critical space for Dare was a worthy pursuit for a dissertation, so she championed the topic."

"I would love to read them," said Calista.

"Happy to loan them to you, but they are my only copies — so you have to promise to return them."

"I swear," Calista said solemnly. "Plus, you know where I live."

Willa raised a finger. "Perhaps you should consider trying to obtain the necessary permissions to publish them in critical editions, to make them available to new readers."

"Isn't that usually done by established scholars?"

"Well, if no one else is doing it . . ." She raised her eyebrows.

"Good point." I had considered something along those lines but never dared to say it out loud.

Simone simpered. "So brave of you, Lila, to take on such an *unknown* author. I chose a regular old traditional writer."

"Who was that?" Willa asked.

"Charlotte Brontë," Simone said. "I couldn't help myself." She blushed prettily. "I'm just back from Haworth, where I immersed myself in all things Brontë-related and I could go on and on about it, but I won't. Obviously, it isn't as groundbreaking as what Lila's doing," she said brightly, "but I guess I'm just an old-fashioned scholar."

"Haworth?" Willa asked, twinkling at Simone. "I'm from a village very close by."

The two of them had a rapid conversation full of landmarks with which I was wholly unfamiliar. Willa asked about the research, and Simone's overview of her *Jane Eyre* project was received with polite interest from the group.

"Well, I love your topic," Tad said firmly. "The truly great never go out of style."

"I think so too," said Simone. "Although it is challenging to find something new to say about someone who has been written about in such volume. It must be far less daunting to write about a brand new author.

Don't you agree, Lila?"

A satisfied look flashed across her face.

Whatever.

"And how did you come to your topic?" Simone pressed, apparently not finished with me. "Was it because of your mother?"

That was a surprise. She must have done some research.

"Your mother?" Tad asked, intrigued.

"Yes, her mother is Violet O." Simone looked around the circle. "You know, the *artist* who specializes in the macabre." I was probably the only one who detected the hint of mockery in her emphasis, but I'd been down this road before.

My mother's provocative show, "True Confessions of the Femme Fatales" had catapulted her into the history books. She often used mystery tropes to explore issues of gender and identity. Initially, my mother's work had been described by critics as "disturbing" and "hysterical," but once she'd made a name for herself, they called it "incisive" and "revolutionary." Take for example her installation, *Cursed:* an enormous silver revolver balanced on black-stockinged legs, looming over a triangular fountain of dark red liquid, surrounded by circular mirrors on which the word "bitch" was scrawled many times in crimson lipstick. Then there was *The Dame Knows Too Much,* a wall-sized canvas of a black and white still from some forgotten noir film, which displayed a victimized woman screaming her head off. Only in my mother's rendition, the woman's head is literally coming off, tilting down from the canvas "in an effort to resist the male gaze," explained my mother to reporters. The lurid soundtrack running nonstop at full volume — combined with the unnatural angle of the woman's broken neck — gave me night-mares for months.

Expressions of surprise and a barrage of questions came straight at me.

Yes, she was The Famous Artist. Yes, her recent *Trench Coat Grotesques* had been the talk of the art world. Yes, she was the one who just gave that controversial interview in *The New York Times.* I went into answer mode until the queries finally — thankfully — subsided.

Simone studied me. I held my breath, expecting her to delve more into the subject of my mother's work. I'd hoped to settle in here at Stonedale, establish myself on my own terms, before having conversations about my mother. I was proud of her, but I'd spent my life to date answering ques-tions about Violet O and her art. Didn't seem to matter that I wasn't the one who made the radical statements: my mother did. But some people felt as though they needed to make a statement about her statements, and Simone had all the characteristics of just such a critic. Instead, however, Simone swerved to the left, launching into an enthusiastic description of how much she already loved the campus, ending with "I'm just so thrilled to be here." Despite my frustration, I was amused by her sugary tone — one degree sweeter and cotton candy might fly out of her mouth.

"What was *that* about?" Calista said under her breath, squeezing my arm. "I was about to jump in and school Simone on the importance of Aunt Vi's work, but you handled it beautifully, Lil."

She gave me a quick hug and went in search of a drink refill. Willa excused herself to find Judith. Simone drifted away, presumably to ingratiate herself with more Stonedale community members. I took a much-needed gulp of red wine.

Nate walked up, in the process of rolling the sleeves of his yellow button-down shirt. "How goes it, my colleagues?"

Tad eyed him affectionately. "Nate, you seem as ebullient as ever. What's your secret? I am in the process of transforming my Byronic brooding into something more socially acceptable and could use some pointers."

Nate grinned and slung an arm around Tad's shoulder. "Just be yourself, man." He gestured to the side table. "And pass the cheese tray. I find that cheese holds the answers to many of life's obstacles."

Tad handed over the small porcelain platter, and Nate speared a few cubes. "See, cheddar is good for when you need a break from grading. And this one here," he peered closely at it, "so gourmet I don't even know what it's called, is very useful when you are in possession of information not widely known yet and are trying not to say anything." He popped it into his mouth and chewed while we badgered him to go on.

Finally, he swallowed and said, "The chancellor came into the department library right after our meeting and said he'd received Spencer's note and would be happy to rearrange the budget for the line so as to hire a temporary replacement for Roland."

That didn't seem quite worth the suspenseful buildup. Tad appeared disappointed as well.

"Yeah, but here's the thing: guess who will be teaching his Shakespeare class?"

We both waited.

"His brother." Nate laughed. "You should see your faces."

"His brother?" Tad repeated, looking stunned.

"Turns out Eldon is a Shakespeare scholar too. Ph.D. from Northwestern, I think." Nate ate another cube of cheese. "The chancellor said that in light of Eldon's forthcoming donation to the university, having him take over the class seemed like a grand idea."

"Even so," said Tad, "I think I need another glass of wine to sip slowly and ponder. Anyone else?"

The two of them trundled across the room to the caterer's bar as I drifted nearer to the main entrance hall, smiling at several of my new colleagues while keeping an eye out for Judith. Perhaps she could offer more insight into this turn of events. Finally, I spotted her beside the staircase. Willa was talking intently and Judith was shaking her head, clearly not agreeing with whatever was being said. I wandered back into the room to give them some privacy and was descended upon at once by Addison, who wore a vague air of abandonment, in contrast to the cheery red bowtie he sported. He inquired about how I was settling in, and we chatted for about ten minutes until Willa invited us to help ourselves to the buffet. Addison joined the line of diners, but I excused myself and went back in quest of Judith.

The hall was empty this time, thankfully. Socializing with new colleagues — no matter how much I liked them — was an exhausting task, and I welcomed the brief moment of respite. I hadn't yet become accustomed to being "on" in the expected way at faculty gatherings. In fact, the transition from grad student, when one could scurry about and not worry about being noticed, to professor, when every gesture, word, or facial expression could potentially disqualify one from obtaining tenure, was fraught with peril.

I hated having to worry about tenure so much, but all new professors did, out of necessity — and there's a constant performance element required. Which made Simone Raleigh rather dangerous. She was unmistakably out for blood, but I didn't have a clue as to why. We barely knew each other. What could I possibly have done to have earned her wrath already?

Willa's encouragement to propose scholarly editions of Isabella Dare's work ran through my mind, and I instinctively grabbed the place where my satchel usually hangs, then glanced around for a pen and slip of paper to jot down some thoughts about securing permissions. I headed down the hallway, pausing at the first door on my right, which was cracked just enough that I could see a bookshelf. Knocking gently, I pushed it open and went into the room. A large desk with a banker's light was directly ahead, and all four walls were lined with bookcases. I let out a whistle of appreciation and moved towards the back wall to read the titles of the books filling every inch of the shelves. After tripping on something and checking to see what it was, I heard a scream and realized dully that it was my own. There, sprawled face down on the luxuriously thick carpet, was Judith.

CHAPTER 8

Once again, I was seated across from Detective Archer. Only this time, we were in Judith's living room with a claw-footed antique table between us. Coffee in bone china cups and saucers with a delicate floral pattern further contributed to the illusion that we were having a chummy social visit. The light seemed overly bright, my head was pounding, and my hands shook. I observed them curiously, wondering if they would stop moving soon.

"Let's begin, Dr. Maclean. I need to take a statement from you." He tapped his pen on the same small black leather pad from our first interview. No first name use today, I noted.

"Have you heard anything about Judith yet?" Although she had still been breathing when the paramedics arrived and loaded her into the back of the ambulance, she didn't seem conscious. The sight of her

101

St. John the Baptist Parish Library
2920 New Hwy. 51
LaPlace, LA 70068

strapped onto the stretcher filled me with a sense of helplessness.

"She's been stabilized."

Relief coursed through my veins. "What happened?"

"Can we talk about what you saw, please?" He practically thrummed with pent-up energy, though that was probably to be expected, given they hadn't yet caught Roland's murderer and now someone else had been attacked.

"Do you think the same person did this?"

"I can't give you any details. But I am interested in you giving *me* some." He waved his pen. "Okay?"

"Okay. I went into the library and found Judith."

He flipped the notepad open to a clean page and waited, pen poised. "Could you tell me what you saw at the party before you went into the library?"

"My colleagues —"

"And they would be?"

"Calista James, Nate Clayton, Tad Ruthersford, Addison Goldman, Judith Westerly, and Willa Hartwell." He recorded the information while I checked my hands, which were still trembling.

"Did anyone seem upset?"

"No. Well — wait. Willa and Judith were

arguing in the hallway."

Archer looked up so quickly that I knew he thought it important. "Arguing? About what?"

"I couldn't hear them. I was passing by and noticed they were in a serious conversation. Willa seemed to be trying to convince Judith of something."

"What was Judith doing when Willa was talking to her?"

"Shaking her head." I realized it sounded as though I were pointing a suspicious finger at Willa. "But, Detective Archer, they are really good friends. I'm sure it was nothing connected to, ah, this." I gestured feebly around the room.

"What happened next?"

"I went back to the party and spoke to Addison until Willa returned."

Archer waited.

"When I came out into the hallway, it was empty."

He watched me intently. "Is that when you went into the library?"

"Yes."

"Why did you go inside?"

"I could see the bookshelves through the door and wanted to get closer . . ."

"To?"

"You know, read the titles." He seemed

skeptical, and I blushed. It was hard to explain to someone who wasn't a bibliophile why a bookshelf might call out to you.

"Did you see Judith at that time?"

"No. I didn't see her at all until I tripped over her. She was beside the desk."

"Did you touch anything?"

"Yes, I went over and felt the pulse in her neck. And put my ear by her mouth to make sure she was breathing. Then I picked up the phone on the desk and called 911."

"But you didn't touch anything else?"

"No." The detective noted that down. "Then I went out in the hallway and yelled for help."

"Who was the first to arrive?"

I closed my eyes, trying to remember. It was difficult to get a clear picture of what had followed the discovery. There were many things happening simultaneously: men and women coming and going — shouting, crying, murmuring. "Spencer Bartholomew, I think. No, wait, it was Willa. They both arrived around the same time."

"What did they do?"

"Willa started to run into the room, but Spencer stopped her, then told me to stand in the doorway, as a barrier, I guess. Then he went over to be with Judith until the ambulance and police arrived. Willa went back into the party and tried to organize people. I heard her saying there had been an accident."

"Can you think of any reason someone might want to hurt Judith?"

"Absolutely not."

"No jealousy in the department?"

"Well, there's always jealousy everywhere, isn't there? But I don't know anything specific. People who've been here longer would, I'm sure."

He regarded me thoughtfully. "I find it hard to believe you've been in Stonedale such a short while and have already found two bodies."

"Bodies? Please don't call Judith a body." The room seemed to spin slightly. I sat up straighter on the sofa to counter the effect.

"I'm serious, Professor. Can you explain your involvement?"

"No. I have no idea what's going on here. But if you're accusing me — *are* you accusing me?"

He was silent.

"You think *I* could have done it? Seriously? I hardly know these people. I don't have any reason."

"Well," he said, as he flipped through his notes. "Judith was your faculty mentor." He went back a few more pages. "And Roland mocked your research in several different instances."

"Yes, Judith and I were becoming friends. She has been kind to me. And yes, Roland was disparaging. But why would I attack my colleagues? I wanted this job more than anything in the world." I was having trouble speaking calmly, battling simultaneous waves of defensiveness and fear.

He shrugged. "How many people do you know who are the first on a crime scene twice in one month?"

"I understand what you're saying. But I didn't *want* to be the first person there."

His lips twitched, as though he was trying not to smile. "Well, you are the only thing linking both scenes so far."

I couldn't move.

"Except for this," he continued. He scribbled something on a page of his notepad and slid it across the table. "Can you identify it?"

I glanced at it. "It looks like a circle with a fence inside it."

He looked down. "I didn't draw it very well. But does it remind you of anything? Do you know what it means?"

"No, I don't know what it means. What is it?" I met his eyes.

"I'm asking what *you* think it means." He

tapped the page.

I examined it more thoroughly. "It just looks like a fence, or rows of letter Xs around something . . . another circle? What is that?"

He shot me an exasperated look. "I'm asking the questions here."

"Right." I took a sip of the coffee in front of me, which was a mistake, as it was both bitter and cold.

He jotted something, then reached down and produced an object encased in a clear plastic bag. He set it on the table, putting on a pair of latex gloves before unzipping the bag and pulling out an enormous book. Silver print against the dark red binding identified it as *Selected Works of Virginia Woolf.* Gently, he lifted the front cover and went to the title page, upon which rested a large embossed symbol. "What's this?"

"Is it what you were drawing?"

He shrugged. "Trying to."

"Wow," I said. It was an intricate design, a circle with what looked like thorny branches crisscrossing around a smaller circle, inside of which was a rosebud. It seemed vaguely familiar, but I couldn't place it.

"What is this doing here?"

I shrugged. "I have no idea how it got there."

"No, I mean why would there be a graphic pressed into the paper?"

"Oh, it's one way to identify a book as belonging to a personal library. Some people write their names in books. Others glue in bookplates or use a special tool — kind of like a metal clamp — to emboss the page, like this. Does the book have anything else embossed? Just a symbol is slightly unusual, though not unheard of."

The detective studied the page briefly, then closed the book and returned it to the plastic. "We'll check it out, thanks."

"Is that Judith's book?"

"What makes you say that?"

"She studies Woolf. Was that in the library? I didn't see it. It's huge."

"Huge enough to knock someone unconscious, at least, wouldn't you say?"

I stared at him. "Someone hit Judith with a book?"

"But since you didn't touch it, we won't find your fingerprints on it, right?"

"No. I already told you. I only touched her neck and the phone." His steady gaze was unnerving. I knew I hadn't done anything, but it made me feel guilty somehow. "You said the rose thing was at the first crime scene too?"

The detective pressed his lips together and

hesitated before nodding.

"Where?"

He went on as if he hadn't heard me. "By the way, Lila, you didn't mention you and Roland had been arguing on the day of his death."

"I wouldn't call it arguing," I said.

"What would you call it?"

I chose my next word carefully. "Conferring."

He waited for me to continue. When I didn't, he sighed. "About what were you conferring?"

"I proposed a class on mysteries, and Roland rejected it."

"Was that all?"

"He also implied I should mind my Ps and Qs."

"Meaning?"

"Meaning I should know my place. Show more deference. Shut up, basically."

"That must have made you angry," he said, in a neutral tone. He sounded like a therapist.

"Of course it did."

Something shifted in his eyes.

"I was angry. But not murderously angry, if that's what you're getting at."

"Why didn't you mention it the first time we talked?"

"I didn't know I was supposed to bring it up. I was answering your questions."

He consulted his notepad. "Did Roland talk to you about anything else that day?"

I thought back. "Yes. My research."

"Tell me more." He had begun taking notes again.

"In Roland's opinion, which he droned on and on about in front of the entire department during my campus interview, by the way, Isabella Dare had three strikes against her. Scholars hadn't written about her, which meant, to him, she could not be of value since everybody important must have already been discovered."

Archer's eyebrows went up.

"That's not true," I informed him. "It's just what Roland believed."

"I got that," he said. "Go ahead."

"So the first strike was that Isabella is an unknown. Second, she wrote mysteries. Popular fiction, to him, had nothing to do with *real* literary studies. Third, she was a woman. Enough said." Just thinking about the way Roland had belittled my work in public infuriated me all over again.

The detective regarded me thoughtfully.

"And yet you continued to work on Isabella."

"Yes."

"Even though you knew your boss would be displeased?"

"Yes, but it's not that simple. It wasn't like I was directly defying an order from my commander or something. Research topics are . . ." I wasn't sure how to end that sentence. "Captivating," I tried. "An original topic is difficult to come by, all-consuming, and nearly impossible to relinquish once you've sunk your teeth into it."

"I see," he said.

"Besides, no one should prevent a professor from working on any subject. In the spirit of academic freedom and all that."

Detective Archer wrote something down, then scrutinized me again. "Is there anything else you'd like to tell me?"

"Just that I didn't mean to cause any problems. I'm trying to do my job. Part of the issue is that Roland and I approached the study of literature very differently."

"Sure sounds like it," he said.

"It's inevitable that there will be conflict in any department. But there's a professional way to handle disagreements. Roland's way is . . ." I stopped and corrected my tense. "Roland's way was demeaning."

"To you?"

"And to others."

"Like? Wait, hold on." Detective Archer

reviewed several pages quickly, his eyes scanning from side to side at a rapid pace. Maybe he'd had speed reader training.

I tried to head him off at the pass. "I don't really want to go into department gossip —"

"Like Tad?"

Unwillingly, I confirmed it, with the smallest possible nod ever.

"What can you tell me about Roland and Tad?"

"It's not really my story to tell," I said. "I only heard that Tad was almost denied tenure because of Roland."

The detective studied my face.

"You know, Dr. Maclean, it would be helpful for you to *volunteer* information that is in any way related to these events."

"Sure," I said. "But that's all I know. It happened last year, and I wasn't even in Stonedale then."

"Is there anything else you can think of that might be pertinent?"

"Not right now."

"Please call me if anything else occurs to you." Archer removed a small white business card from his pocket and pushed it across the coffee table at me.

"I will," I assured him as I picked it up.

"We may need to talk with you again."

"That's fine. I'm not going anywhere." I looped the strap of my bag across my body and stood.

He held up a finger. "One more question, Lila. What reasons might your cousin have for being involved in any of this?"

"Calista's not involved. She would never do something to hurt another person. Why would you think that?"

Neither of us spoke while his blue eyes searched mine. Finally, he sighed and said I was free to go.

On the way home, I stopped by the hospital, but since I wasn't family, they wouldn't let me see Judith yet. So instead I spent a quiet night flipping channels while going over the events of the evening in my mind. Calista called late, asking about my interview. We compared notes, as she had also been asked to give a statement, but Detective Archer must have used different strategies for different people, as she was shocked to hear the weapon had been a book.

"It was a *Woolf* book?" She sounded oddly intense.

"Yes, does that mean something? Do you know if it was Judith's?"

"I . . . I don't know. She has a ton of Woolf books, but I'm not sure if that was one of them. What did it look like?"

"It was red with silver lettering, and it had something embossed into the title page. A rosebud with thorns around it."

"Hmm." There was a long pause.

"He asked me if there was any reason for you to be involved."

"What? Of course not. Lila, you know that, right?"

"I do, Cal. I told him so. Did you tell him about your lost knife?"

"I did," she said quickly.

"What did he say?"

"That he wished I'd told him sooner."

"Does he think there's a connection?"

"Well, since the book symbol you described matches the one on my knife, I bet he does."

That was new information. "Wait, that's what was on your knife? You didn't specify before. Where did it come from?"

"A friend gave it to me. Let's leave it at that. I don't want to get anyone in trouble."

"But your friend might be a murderer —"

"That's impossible."

Now I was confused and said so. She was unwilling to provide any additional details, even though I pushed for more information. We agreed to check in later and ended the call. All night, I wondered whom she felt compelled to protect and — what seemed even more incomprehensible — why she wouldn't confide in me about it.

Resolving to stop attempting to figure out the citizens of Stonedale University for a bit, I threw myself into work mode. I stayed up half the night, but cooler weather tends to increase my energy for some reason, and I caught up on all of my grading, a victory in and of itself. On top of that, I managed to draft a very rough book proposal on the Isabella Dare project. It was one thing to understand the requirement to publish — the minimum expected of any tenure-track candidate — but it was a whole other matter to actually put something in writing for submission. Anything on paper was cause for celebration. I still needed to do more research, but at least I had a starting point.

On Monday morning, as I was locking the front door, Tad came out of his house in a black blazer over a crisp white shirt paired with jeans and Doc Martens — very Hip Young Professor. We headed to campus, our shoes crushing the scattered leaves on the sidewalk. I loved when the smothering heat of summer gave way to a properly autumnal crispness and it seemed to have taken even longer to arrive out west, so I was especially grateful this year. I tried to enjoy the moment, even though Judith's welfare was weighing on my mind.

"Have you heard anything about Judith?" I asked Tad.

"Nothing. What did the detective tell you last night? I saw him talking to you."

"Just that she was unconscious and they had stabilized her."

He nodded and we walked silently for a few minutes, then I asked how his conversation with the police went.

He swallowed hard before answering. "That detective was really interested in my relationship with Roland, unfortunately. It's impossible to tell that story without making myself look like an ass. He knew everything already, of course, and was going to talk to me even if someone hadn't attacked Judith. It just made it more convenient for him — and more suspicious for me — that I was in attendance last night."

"But he didn't accuse you of anything, right?" As soon as I asked, I realized it wasn't just me under scrutiny — or Calista, for that matter. The detective had all of us on his suspect list, and he would continue to investigate until someone confessed, or until the truth came out. Which was his job,

I guess, but it was disconcerting all the same.

"Not outright. He seemed disbelieving, though, when I told him I harbored no ill will whatsoever for Judith. She's been nothing but kind to me."

"Me too. Extremely so."

He sighed.

"I hate that the tenure thing has cast such a long shadow over everything. Stonedale was the perfect fit for me before that happened. Now I can see pity in people's faces."

"But that will fade, Tad. And are you sure it's pity? I think it might be sympathy — from what I've heard, everyone believes Roland was not justified in his complaints."

"That's good to hear, but I can't help feeling mortified." He kicked at a small cluster of red and yellow leaves at the edge of the sidewalk.

"I understand. That reminds me — you seemed upset when you came out of Roland's office the other day."

"The day he died?"

I nodded.

"That was bad timing, wasn't it?" He grimaced. "The detective seemed to find it very significant as well. In fact, with that incident plus last year's tenure battle, I'm surprised they haven't hauled me into jail yet. If I didn't know better, I'd suspect myself too."

I didn't know what to say to that.

"But back to Roland's office, it was nothing. I gave him a copy of my book, he insulted me, and I left."

"Congratulations on the book!" I applauded him briefly. "Is it on Defoe?"

"Yes," he said, cheering up. "Came out this summer. It was actually in the editing stages when I went up for tenure last year, but Roland wouldn't let me count it because it wasn't published yet."

"That seems unfair," I said. "Don't they usually count books in process for tenure if you have a contract?"

"Not at Stonedale, evidently. Or at least in our department. Anyway, professors are expected to give the department a copy to display on the bookshelf in the main office. So I handed it to him and he made some comment about how the university press that had published it had fallen in stature. He followed that up with a jab about how no one was really working on Defoe anymore."

"What a jerk," I said, remembering how Roland had flung the book onto Millicent's desk and told her to file it. I'd been surprised he threw it — not usual behavior from people who love literature. But now it made more sense: not only was he going to disrespect the book, but also Tad himself by not including it in the front office display.

Tad shrugged. "Par for the Roland Higgins course. I just hope the detective puts it into proper perspective."

"I had an argument with Roland too, right after you." It was more of a standoff than an argument, technically, but still.

"I heard about that. Good for you. What did the detective say?"

"He didn't understand why I would keep researching something my boss didn't approve of."

"He doesn't understand academia, then," said Tad, with an eye roll.

"Clearly not," I agreed. "What are you teaching today?"

He brightened. "*A Journal of the Plague Year.*

"Oh, and Defoe is your person, so there's that."

"True indeed. Will you be able to teach your, um, person this semester?"

"Isabella? Hadn't thought of doing that, but perhaps I should. I didn't assign her books — they are way out of print — but I could project excerpts and introduce her work to my Gothic Lit class. Thanks, Tad."

"Happy to help."

When we reached Crandall, he bid me goodbye, but not before telling me to be careful. I knew what he meant; with two English professor attacks in a row, probably the entire faculty was on edge right about now.

After my classes and office hours, I headed over to the hospital. This time, the nurse at the desk gave me Judith's room number. As I walked down the blindingly white hallway, I sniffed the wildflowers I'd brought with me, trying to block the antiseptic tang in the air. At the sign for room 240, I knocked on the door.

"Come in," called Judith. Her voice sounded cheerful and strong — not what I'd expected at all.

I walked around the curtain and found her propped up by several pillows, surrounded by books and papers. She smiled and gestured to an empty chair next to her bed.

I sat down and handed her the flowers.

She put the bouquet to her nose. "How sweet of you. These are exquisite and have lifted my spirits already. Now tell me how you are doing."

"No, I want to hear about you. How are

you?" Her color seemed normal, which I was glad to see, and her natural elegance made the hospital gown almost graceful.

"Pshaw," she said, waving dismissively. "I'm absolutely fine. In fact, I'm going home in a few hours. They just wanted to keep me here for observation given the," she leaned forward and said in a mocking tone, "seriousness of the attack."

"But Judith, it *was* serious. Someone hurt you."

"I know, I shouldn't jest, but it was a book, not an ax."

"A heavy book."

"And probably symbolic, though I can't imagine who would want me to be knocked out by my own research topic." She chuckled. "Then again, Virginia has always been able to get under the skin of some people."

I squeezed her hand briefly. "I'm just glad you're okay."

"Thank you, dear, I do appreciate your concern."

"Did you see who hit you?"

"No . . . I can't remember anything after walking into the room. Don't even remember why I went into the room in the first place." She patted my hand. "But don't worry yourself about it."

"I can't help worrying, Judith."

"I would certainly be worrying far more if they hadn't given me some divine medicine that has whisked my cares away," she said.

I suppose that explained her current state of serenity, which I found somewhat unsettling. "Do you mind if I ask you something about the book?"

"Not at all."

"There was a symbol embossed in the front — with thorns or something."

"How interesting."

"Do you know what it means?"

"Sorry, dear. It wasn't my book."

"But it was Woolf."

"Nonetheless," Judith said. "It wasn't mine. People all over the world own Virginia's books. And it is a fine and glorious thing that they do."

"Of course. I'm just trying to . . . connect the dots."

Judith plucked at a seam on the hospital blanket thoughtfully. Eventually, she looked up and smiled at me kindly. "I'm sure the police will make sense of it."

Although I had never found Judith to be anything but forthright, I couldn't help but feel that she was holding something back.

CHAPTER 9

A few weeks later, we were all gathered in the department library again for the monthly faculty meeting. As I waited for the meeting to be called to order, I surveyed the roomful of my new colleagues, wondering if one of them could possibly be a murderer. It was almost intolerable to imagine, but someone had killed Roland and attacked Judith. Fighting a deep sense of unease, I tried to read the minutes from our last meeting, but the words didn't organize themselves into any sort of meaning.

Spencer consulted the agenda in front of him. "I'd like to begin by welcoming Dr. Eldon Higgins, who will be teaching Roland's Shakespeare course for the remainder of the term. We are most grateful to you, Dr. Higgins, for coming to our assistance. Your brother, as you know, was an active and important member of our department, and we gladly anticipate getting to know you better over the coming months."

We all murmured welcomes in Eldon's direction, and he produced a pained squint and a slight dip of the head in response. I wondered how Eldon and Roland had developed such an air of self-importance. Or perhaps it was a defense mechanism — I'd met enough academics to know that pomposity often grew from a carefully buried sense of worthlessness. On the other hand, some professors did actually believe in their own intellectual superiority. It was difficult to sort out who belonged to which category.

Willa, resplendent in a gleaming steel-colored tunic and armful of silver bangles, addressed Spencer. "Are we ready to vote on the History of Drama course?"

"Thanks for the reminder, Willa. Let's review the materials."

She passed around a pile of handouts and invited us to read them. "This is a revised version of the syllabus we discussed at length last spring. Thanks for your suggestions — you'll see we have incorporated many of them."

Eldon, clad in the same tweedy garb his brother had favored, wiggled his fingers delicately. "May I ask what some of the changes are?"

"Of course." Willa walked him through the list of assigned texts.

"There are, if you don't mind my saying so, more female authors on here than I've seen in traditional survey courses," said Eldon.

Willa nodded. "That was one of our goals, actually — more diversity in terms of gender and ethnicity."

"But certainly we needn't add female playwrights simply because they are female. I see you've only included one play each by some of the more prominent male playwrights, and obviously that's problematic."

"Well, Eldon," Willa said, "putting aside for now the reductive quality of your objection, that a writer would be added 'simply,' as you say, because of their gendered position, let us proceed on the understanding that we wanted the course to be more inclusive."

He snorted. "Typical. My brother was always quite indignant about the clamoring to celebrate every Jill or Jane who picked up a pen. But, and I have to say I agree with him, that would do an injustice to the illustrious genius of the existing members of the canon."

Calista shook her head, but she remained

quiet amidst the mutters around the table.

Willa ventured forward with a steady approach. "Dr. Higgins, feminist scholarship has an important place in our curricular goals."

"I've heard all the arguments, Willa. And I'm extraordinarily tired of the need to harp on such things —"

"Speaking is not harping," Willa interjected calmly.

Eldon waved at that, as if shooing a fly. "An unfortunate choice of words, then. But let us acknowledge there are statistics —"

"Yes, we all have statistics, but I predict you will posit that mine are somehow flawed and yours are not." She stared him down.

"It's not a matter of gender," Eldon said, "but a question of significance, as my brother used to say."

Willa tapped the table briskly. "That's part of the problem. It *can* be about gender. Too often, we are served up literary forefathers for the main course, and when a woman writer is discussed, she is presented as the soufflé that fell a little flat: she is too sentimental, too realistic, too restrained, too strident — it's always too *something.*"

Eldon shifted in his chair and brushed a small speck off of his vest. "Perhaps you need to be more objective, Willa. If some of the women writers simply aren't as good, then we shouldn't feel bad that we prefer the men."

"Just because you 'prefer' certain writers doesn't mean that everyone else is unnecessary." Willa was gripping the edge of the conference table so hard that her knuckles were white. "At least admit that a general lack of representation has been an issue. I'm not saying ignore the men — I'm saying include the women."

He leaned back, looking smug. "It's an outdated stand. We're in an era of post-feminism now. Hasn't the news reached the west?"

"Post-post feminism," Norton chimed in gleefully.

Eldon nodded at the contribution.

Willa threw up her hands, the bracelets jangling atonally. "Anyone can make pronouncements. Meanwhile, women are out in the world, experiencing what people claim is not happening, which is one of the most dangerous aspects of this mess."

Her glare was fierce.

Eldon's left eye twitched.

Judith called for a vote on the matter at hand. The course passed, with everyone voting for it except Eldon and Norton. No surprise there, though I was taken aback at the sheer audacity of Eldon's decision to make a political attack on the curriculum in front of the entire faculty. Chancellor Wellington must have assured him that the forthcoming donation granted him an immunity of sorts. Otherwise, I couldn't imagine a new colleague, however temporary, taking such a chance.

Outside, on the bench in front of Crandall Hall, I asked Calista and Nate if they had any ideas about why Spencer, as interim department chair, hadn't stepped in to take control of the escalating situation.

She rolled her eyes. "I know, right? What was that about?"

Nate looked thoughtful.

"Maybe he didn't want to embarrass Eldon on his first day. And don't forget — there is the donation factor, which secured Eldon the job, by all accounts."

"But still, he just let him go on and on —" Calista broke off upon the realization that Willa had joined us and leaped up to hug her. "How are you? That was just awful. But you were absolutely amazing in there."

I agreed enthusiastically.

"Bravo," said Nate. "You sure know how to command a room."

Willa laughed. "Thank you all. Rest assured, I've been involved in worse battles. At least the course was passed and Eldon showed us where he stands. I will claim it as a victory."

The door opened, and I could hear low voices. Norton and Eldon emerged, deep in conversation.

"Time to leave," Willa said, and we did.

An hour later, Calista and I were sitting on her back porch in a pair of brown wicker chairs topped with soft yellow cushions. I took another drink of the pomegranate concoction she'd made in the blender and sighed happily. It was tangy and cold and hit the proverbial spot. We were making short work of the platter of crackers and cheese on the small wicker table between us as we watched the sun go down over her back fence.

"Do you have a lot of grading to do this weekend?" she asked.

"Heaps. But could we talk about the department meeting? What was Eldon thinking?"

"Don't know. I think we were all in shock. Otherwise Judith probably would have spoken up. She's usually superb at defusing angry situations."

"She is?"

"Seriously gifted. Last year, Judith and I were talking in my office when Spencer and Roland had the loudest argument in the hallway — I don't know what it was about because they were yelling at the same time so it was hard to distinguish words. Judith heard the ruckus, excused herself and within two minutes, the three of them were laughing together about something. Then she returned and we took up where we left off, as if nothing had happened."

I was impressed. "What, did she cast a spell?"

She laughed. "Hmm. If Judith were a witch, it would explain a lot."

"What do you mean?"

Calista shrugged. "She's just a very powerful woman."

A loud knock at the front door startled us both. She sighed and put down her drink. I stayed where I was as she went to answer, enjoying the sight of the sky over the Rocky Mountains, which comprised varying shades of blue and red tinged with gold.

Noticing that my glass was empty, I wandered into the house to seek a refill. Stepping through her sliding glass door, I stopped short. Police were everywhere, searching through cabinets and drawers.

Calista was sitting on her sofa, talking with Detective Archer. I headed straight for them.

"What's going on?"

Calista looked up, her expression grim. "They're searching my house. And arresting me."

"For what?" My head swiveled towards the detective, whose mouth was set in a straight line. "This is a mistake. She didn't do anything," I said to him, directly. I didn't care what he did to me for speaking up.

"I'm going to have to ask you to sit over there, Dr. Maclean. I'll be with you shortly." He pointed at a chair in the dining area.

I did as he said, watching the police personnel come and go. A half hour passed, during which they carried out Calista's laptop, briefcase, and several boxes of files. At one point, Cady shot across the room and hid under the legs of my chair. I picked up the cat and cradled her in my arms, making soothing sounds.

Eventually, two officers went over to Calista and asked her to stand up. She followed their directions, turning around so that they could apply the handcuffs. As they took her out to the patrol car, she yelled for me to take care of Cady.

Detective Archer approached me, all business, tucking the small notepad into his chest pocket. I stayed in the chair and focused on petting the cat slowly to ground myself against the lurching of my stomach. Also to ignore him for as long as possible.

He leaned his arms on the table.

"We're done here," he said softly. "Can you lock up?"

"Yes. What happens now?"

"She'll be processed. I wouldn't expect to hear anything today, but you'll be able to see her soon enough. By Monday at the latest."

I nodded.

"You'll be responsible for the cat?"

I was battling a potent cocktail of anger and disbelief, and I couldn't seem to get my thoughts straight. "Yes."

He studied my face, assessing something, I didn't know what, then left.

The house seemed especially quiet in comparison to the recent chaos. I went around closing drawers, picking up and righting things. It only took a few minutes to locate the cat carrier and food in the garage, but a good twenty more to cajole Cady out from under Calista's bed, where she had retreated after the police left. Thank goodness for the tempting powers of catnip.

Cady meowed when I scooped her up, but

she didn't claw me. I explained that she was going to stay with me for a while, then set her carefully inside the carrier. I'd heard many stories about cats protesting their carriers, but Cady curled up neatly and stared impassively through the bars of the door. I couldn't help noting the symbolism and hoped Calista was as calm about her own incarceration, though I doubted it.

CHAPTER 10

On Saturday, I drove first to the Stonedale police station, then to the jail, trying to get some answers, but no one would let me see Calista.

All weekend, I phoned the jail for more information — each time, they told me to be patient, to wait to hear from her. I tried to prepare classes and grade, but the worry shattered my ability to concentrate, and I resorted to pacing around my house and talking to my mother on my cell. She checked for updates every few hours, and we speculated until we both felt sick. On Sunday evening, Calista finally called and said I could visit her the next day.

I awoke slowly Monday, swimming up to consciousness gradually, as if I'd been drugged. Obviously the stress was doing strange things to me. I raced through my morning routine and walked to campus, veering at the last minute to go by the coffee shop in the student union. If ever there was a time I needed a bolster of caffeine, it was now.

Joining the long line in front of the counter, I pulled out my cell phone to check my email. I scrolled through the list of student emails and campus announcements, responding to whatever needed it. Soon, I became aware of familiar voices ahead of me and looked up to see Eldon and Norton conversing. The man between us was extremely tall as well as broad, so he provided a perfect wall of camouflage. I quickly ducked my head again and tried to zero in on what they were saying.

"It was in Roland's file," said Norton. "Right there in black and white."

Eldon made a strange wheezing sound, which I eventually realized was a laugh.

"Of course I called the detective," Norton continued. "And that was that."

"I wouldn't count my eggs before they hatched," Eldon warned him.

"This egg is a golden one. I'm quite sure."

"Well, good luck. I know you feel strongly about this."

"I do indeed," said Norton, with a nasty cackle.

Clearly they were talking about the case since they'd mentioned the detective. Before

I knew what I was doing, I'd stepped around the person in front of me — murmuring "I just want to say hi really quick" — and faced both of my colleagues.

Norton's jaw dropped, but he recovered quickly.

"Good morning, gentlemen," I said. "What are we talking about?"

"Nothing that concerns you," muttered Norton.

"Sorry to interrupt," I said. "But I'm just beside myself today, with what's happened to my cousin, and I wondered if you had any ideas about what's going on."

I was gratified to see color rise in Eldon's cheeks, though he didn't speak.

"Did I hear something about an egg?"

Norton pulled out his antique pipe and sucked on the mouthpiece for a moment. I could tell he was trying to decide what to say next.

"We were talking about ordering breakfast," he said finally. But there was something regretful in his voice, as if he'd lost an opportunity to crow.

I waited for him to say more.

No one spoke. A minute passed by, then another, during which we shuffled silently forward as a unit, ever closer to the counter. It was excruciatingly awkward, and eventually there was nothing left to do but return to my place in line.

I drank deeply from my grande latte on the way to class. Within minutes, the caffeine restored me, and I walked a bit more briskly, turning my thoughts to the questions I'd be asking the students to discuss.

I was so lost in my planning that I didn't register who was walking in front of me at first. Once again, it was Norton, but he was talking to Addison this time. I quickened my pace, hoping to hear them while still remaining far enough behind to be unobtrusive. As we passed the fountain, they raised their voices to counter the splashing water.

"— but I don't understand why you called the detective," said Addison.

"Because she did it," Norton said, sounding exasperated. "Plain and simple."

"Had she seen it, though?" Addison stopped walking abruptly and turned to look at his companion. I slowed down too.

"Doesn't matter," Norton replied. "She knew what was coming. And that, my friend, is more than enough."

"I think it does matter." I cheered inwardly that Addison was not simply buying what Norton was selling. He appeared to have more of a spine than he was generally credited with.

I hurried to catch up to them, greeted Addison warmly, then asked Norton if I could have a word. I sounded polite, even though we both knew I was going to talk to him with or without his permission.

Norton gave me a curt nod. The two of them made plans to meet later. I waited until Addison's tall frame had plodded across to the far sidewalk, then I spun around to face Norton.

"I couldn't help overhearing your conversation —"

He fixed me with a glare. "The second time in one day? Are you stalking me?"

"Not at all."

"What do you want, then?"

I made an effort to soften my tone. "Could you please tell me what you gave to the detective?"

He fumbled in his pocket, pulled out and lit his pipe, and took a long draw. As he let the acrid smoke out, he watched me out of the corner of his eye. Then his lip curled into a sneer. "Motive. Your cousin killed my friend. I was glad to provide evidence to that effect."

"We're going to have to agree to disagree about the killing part, but what is the evidence?" I plastered on a smile, trying to stay calm.

He laughed, a brittle and unpleasant sound. "You are not a tenured professor, Dr. Maclean. You are not on the tenure committee. So all I can say to you is that there is formal written evidence. You do the math."

Norton smirked, clearly feeling as though he'd put me in my place, and stalked away, puffing on his pipe.

But he'd said enough to confirm my suspicions. He was talking about Roland's negative letter about Calista's tenure bid. He'd found it and given it to the detective as "proof" of her guilt.

After class, I was on my way to see my cousin. I stopped by the department to check both of our mailboxes first. I wasn't sure if she would want her mail or not, but the least I could do was bring an offering. A touch of normalcy amid what was probably the least normal environment she'd ever been in.

A crowd of students quieted and dispersed rather pointedly as I made my way down the hallway. Probably talking about Calista. News like a professor's arrest would surely have swept the campus already.

Just when I'd reached the main office,

Nate walked through the door. He took one look at my face and pulled me over to the far wall for privacy.

"I heard," he said. "I'm so sorry."

I fought back the tears that had unexpectedly rushed to my eyes. "I can't believe this is happening."

"How is she doing?" His gaze was full of concern.

"I'm going to see her now. She's not doing well, but at least she can have visitors."

"Do you know why they arrested her?"

I shook my head. "I mean, the knife that killed Roland was hers — you knew that, right?"

"Yes, that came through the grapevine quickly. Is that enough?"

I shrugged. "They may have more. I don't know." I didn't want to talk about the tenure letter in the department until I knew what we were dealing with.

He patted my shoulder somewhat awkwardly. "Keep me posted. And if there's anything I can do, call me immediately."

"Thanks, Nate." I promised to let him know what I found out.

He took a few steps, then turned back to look at me over his shoulder. "I mean it, Lila, call me anytime. Okay?"

"Okay."

I crossed the hall, stepped into the office, and greeted my colleagues. Millicent was typing on the computer keyboard so fast that her hands almost blurred, Eldon was looking over her shoulder at the computer screen and giving directions, and Spencer was sitting in the chair next to her desk, listening intently to whatever it was Eldon was saying about his Shakespeare course. They were so immersed in what they were doing that I needn't have bothered saying hello, but their lack of response was fine with me. I wasn't up to fielding any questions about my cousin, anyway.

I gathered the materials in both of our mailboxes and went into the empty hallway to sort them. An academic journal and several flyers for Calista went into my bag. Matching flyers and student papers for me soon followed, but I paused to rip open a small yellow padded envelope with my name written on it on block letters.

Inside, there was a single sheet of heavy white stock. I unfolded the paper and read the printed words instructing me to wear the enclosed necklace the next time I saw Calista, followed by "Tell no one else."

Perplexed, I looked into the envelope and saw a coiling of chain at the bottom, which I pulled out. The silver necklace had a round disk attached, engraved with the same emblem that had been on the book the detective showed me, featuring interwoven thorny branches around a rose. What the heck?

Calista sat down across from me. Her face seemed paler and thinner than usual, possibly a combination of the orange jumpsuit and the florescent lights. She picked up the black phone attached to the wall.

I did the same. The mouthpiece had a top note of antiseptic, but I caught a whiff of stale breath underneath. I held it a little farther away than was comfortable for my wrist, but it seemed the lesser of two evils.

"How are you?" I asked her.

"Hanging in there," she said. "Thanks for coming to see me. How's Cady?"

"She's fine. I'll take good care of her until you're out. Which will be soon, I hope."

"Since the judge refused to set bail, it depends on when the trial is."

"Why did he refuse it?" That didn't bode well.

"He was a friend of Roland's. He said the monstrous nature of this crime warranted a denial." My cousin's expression was solemn. "You know I didn't do it, right, Lil?"

"Of course. And I'm going to try to figure

out who did."

"I don't know how."

"Well, I can gather information. I'm a scholar. It's what I do." At her dubious air, I went on. "Put it this way: if I don't do something, I'll go crazy.

She gave me a small smile.

"Listen, I overheard Norton talking about a letter that gives you motive. He means Roland's, right?"

"Surely. I told you Roland made it clear the letter wasn't going to be positive."

"Yes, but if you didn't even see it, how could it provide motive?"

"I don't know. Maybe just the fact that Roland told me about it is sufficient?"

"Does the detective know he told you about it?"

"Yes. I really didn't think I had anything to hide."

We stared at each other for a long moment.

"Well, if we're going to get you out of here, we need to find some other suspects pronto. Just between us, who is capable of killing Roland?"

Calista's eyebrows shot up. "I don't want to think anyone at Stonedale could have done this."

"I don't either, but we know you didn't

do it, so we need to come up with someone else the police can look at. If you *had* to choose a colleague, who would it be?"

She studied the ceiling, pursing her lips. "That's a really hard question."

"I mean, the most obvious person might be Tad, given all of his tenure stuff."

"True, but Tad isn't the most assertive person in the world."

Not exactly an iron-clad alibi. "Maybe he was overcompensating for that lack of assertiveness by stabbing Roland?"

"I doubt it. He's from the type of people who use money to fight things, rather than fists."

Not crossing him off of my list yet.

"What about Willa?"

"Not in a million years." She set her jaw. "I understand you haven't known these people very long, but they're my friends."

"Fair enough. Sorry. I just don't know anyone well enough to think through this myself. Should we stop?"

"No. It's weirdly comforting to articulate why I don't think my friends are murderers." Calista studied a fingernail on her hand as she thought. "Although if anyone should have had a grudge against Roland — aside from Tad — it was Willa."

"What do you mean?"

"He always seemed like he was out to get her in public. Ever since I've been here, anyway, whenever she tried to present something to the department, he always mocked it."

"Like Eldon did?"

"Yes, but he was nothing compared to Roland, who was much more contemptuous."

"What did Willa do?"

"She held her own, of course, but it was unbearable."

"Couldn't she have brought a formal complaint against Roland?" I didn't know how Willa managed to keep working with him. It sounded like an awful situation.

"Yes, but that's not her style. She prefers to confront people directly, without involving the administration. Though at one point, they were both called into the dean's office because a faculty member from another department reported that the business of some university committee was being affected by Roland's outbursts towards Willa, but as far as I know, nothing official happened."

"So could she have snapped, after all the years of poor treatment?"

We both pondered this. Finally, Calista said quietly, "I just can't imagine it. She's all about righting wrongs, especially those having to do with equality. I don't know if you know this, but she's made quite a name for herself in academic scholarship. In fact, that may be one of the reasons Roland had it in for her. I think he was jealous of her success."

Ah, jealousy. Now there was a motive. Unfortunately, it was the victim's. We needed one for the killer. "What about Addison? They were close friends, right?"

"Yes, but c'mon. Addy a murderer?"

We shared a smile through the glass. The very idea was preposterous. Addison was the sort of person who would stop traffic to let a ladybug cross the street.

"How about Norton? If I were forced to vote for someone in a murderer poll, he would be my most likely candidate."

Calista rolled her eyes. "He is hostile. No question there. But he and Roland were allies, so it wouldn't make any sense."

I was worried we were going to run out of time, so I started speaking more quickly, even though I felt like I was grasping at straws.

"How about the woman you mentioned before, who was friends with Roland but stopped speaking to him?"

"Elisabetta Vega?"

I nodded.

Calista rejected the idea outright. "Elisabetta is always opinionated — in a necessary way, if you know what I mean — but she is a very compassionate person. She would never kill someone."

"Alright, do you think Spencer was competitive enough to have done something? I mean, he hardly seems a likely villain from what I've seen, but you did mention their history."

"Their competition was more academic than personal."

"But didn't Spencer back Tad in the tenure battle?"

"That's true. But that's because he is a principled, good person. He stood up for Tad because it was the right thing to do, and deep down, I think Roland knew that."

"Do you trust Judith?"

"With my life. Plus, she was just attacked. That makes her a victim."

"Just to play devil's advocate here, she was hit with a book. Couldn't she have thrown it into the air on top of herself?"

Calista shook her head vehemently. "No way."

"Okay, presuming she was attacked, who would do that?"

"I can't think of anyone. She is one of the best people you could ever meet."

Something occurred to me. "You know, Roland's killer and Judith's attacker might not even be the same person . . ."

She sat up straight and considered this. "You're right. Just because they happened close to each other doesn't automatically mean they're connected."

"Who could have wanted to hurt Judith?"

She sighed. "No idea. She's adored by everyone."

I suddenly remembered the necklace, which I'd worn tucked inside my shirt. I pulled it out and showed it to her.

Her face grew even paler, if that was possible.

"Where did you get that? Put it away," she said, flapping her hand urgently. "Right now."

"Someone put it in my mailbox," I said. "Isn't it the same decoration from the book and the knife? What is it?"

She closed her eyes briefly. "I can't tell you. But keep it hidden."

"Why? What does it mean?"

Calista looked down at the table.

I pulled out the letter and pressed it up against the glass so she could read it. "This note was in the same envelope. Can you make any sense of it?"

She scanned it quickly and shook her head.

"Why won't you tell me what that symbol means?"

"I'm sorry — I just can't. I have no idea why you were asked to wear the necklace here. But do *not* show it around, please. You have to trust me, Lil."

A buzzer sounded. I knew that was our cue to say goodbye. "Love you. Be strong."

"You too," she said, before hanging up the phone.

The prisoners stood, almost in unison. Calista turned sideways and gave me an apologetic look before filing out of the room with them.

I watched her, depressed at the thought of her staying in here one minute longer and confused about why, even now, she was keeping secrets.

That night, I took a picture of the necklace with my cell phone, emailed it to myself, and searched for it on Google.

Nothing.

Then I tried doing a search on different variations of roses and thorns, which brought up hundreds of images ranging from illustrations of Sleeping Beauty's castle to tattoo galleries. Apparently, thorny roses were very popular as body art. A few of the folktale illustrations were similar, though not identical, to the image on the necklace, where the thorny branches were stylized: the interlocked twists and turns created a beautifully ornate pattern. The rosebud at the center of the design was simple in contrast, just a spiral to indicate petal tops, with a single curved line forming a cup shape beneath.

I leaned back in the chair and thought. Why would someone want me to wear a necklace with this symbol during a visit with Calista? And why would she then refuse to tell me what it meant? I had the feeling I was playing a role in some game that I didn't understand, and I didn't like it one bit.

On top of that, I definitely needed to find out what Roland's letter said.

I picked up the phone and called Detective Archer.

An hour later, the detective sat at my dining room table. I'd made him some coffee, which steamed silently next to his elbow. I had an urge to move it closer to the center of the table so he wouldn't jostle it by mistake, but I refrained.

He opened his trusty notepad. "I understand this is all very troubling, and I appreciate your offer to talk further about the case. What's the new information you have?"

"Well, it happened a little while ago, but I didn't think it was important until now."

The detective turned to a fresh page and positioned his pen over it. "Go on."

He started writing as I spoke. "When Calista and I were leaving Roland's memorial service, Norton Smythe came barreling over all upset. He said he knew Calista had killed Roland and that she would pay for it."

The detective narrowed his eyes slightly.

"Don't you see? He promised to take revenge. And I heard he gave you a letter that provided some sort of motive."

His lack of reaction was extremely frustrating. But he did appear to be listening, so I kept going.

"Is that why you arrested her?"

"We are not going to talk about that," Archer said decisively, slicing his hand sideways through the air. "And what Dr. Smythe may or may not have said is not part of this discussion."

"But I believe he's trying to frame my cousin." There, I said it. "What does the letter say? It's her tenure letter, right?"

He let the hand holding the pen fall to the table and shifted positions. "I can't talk about that."

"Detective, please listen. I'm sure it's a false clue. I don't think she ever saw it."

He set the notepad down and took a long drink of coffee. "What makes you think that?"

"I asked her."

He nodded and resumed making notes.

"It might not even have been written by Roland. How do we know it came from him? Did someone actually see him write it?" I was determined to cast as much doubt on this letter as possible.

Archer sighed. "As I said, I cannot discuss the letter. Let me ask you something, though. Did your cousin ever talk to you about her knife?"

I tapped the table top for emphasis. "Yes, and that's another part of this. Calista told me Norton stopped by her office and, while he was there, he saw the knife on her desk."

He squinted at me, the fine lines emanating out from the corners of his eyes bringing to mind a young Clint Eastwood. "Why would she tell you Norton saw the knife on her desk?"

"Because after Roland was found, she realized her knife was missing, and she was worried. She was trying to decide when to tell you —"

"The correct answer is right away," he interjected sternly. "For future reference."

"I told her that too. Anyway, that's why he is accusing her. He doesn't know that the knife had been stolen."

Archer wrote something down. "Did he say anything to her about it?"

"Not until the memorial service, I don't think. By then, he'd already made up his mind that she was guilty."

He looked out the window. Or maybe at his reflection in the dark glass. I couldn't interpret his expression.

"Maybe Norton killed Roland," I said. "Otherwise, why would he be so insistent that Calista did it?"

The detective slowly turned his head towards me. "Because he thinks she did."

CHAPTER 11

Cousin in jail or not, I still had a job to do. The room was already full when I arrived a few minutes before the start time of my Gothic class on Wednesday. After organizing my notes, I greeted the students and asked how the assigned reading — Ambrose Bierce's "The Damned Thing" and Edith Wharton's "The Eyes" — had gone for them.

"Creepy," one of the men in the front row said, letting out a low whistle. He was a consistently strong contributor and it wasn't a surprise that he was the first to respond.

Heads nodded in agreement around the room.

"Could you please talk a little more about what you mean, Alex?" I prompted.

He carefully tucked his long sun-streaked hair behind his ears before beginning. "Wharton's eyes, following that guy? I could *see* them."

"Me too," said another student from beneath a thick curtain of brown bangs. She readjusted her position in the seat. "I even had nightmares about them later."

"Sorry about that, Fiona," I said. "It is a disturbing story, for sure. Let's start with Wharton, then. What is it about the eyes that makes them so effective?"

A long discussion followed, during which we explored various technical and symbolic elements.

Alex raised his hand again. "Dr. Maclean, can we talk about the Bierce story now?" At my nod of agreement, he continued, "I can't figure out why he never explains the invisible threat. Freaked me out."

"Yes, how *does* Bierce elicit our strong response, given that he doesn't identify what the 'thing' is?"

"That's what makes it so scary," Fiona said. "You hear about it, and you see results of its existence, but you don't really get a good look at it, like in *The Blair Witch Project*." We spent a good bit of time reviewing the ways in which the film was like the Bierce story, then she made several connections to Gothic conventions we'd been exploring during the semester so far.

"But what if someone didn't know the conventions?" the blonde student sitting next to Fiona protested. She put her black glasses on the desk. "I mean, does it really matter whether or not the person knows it's Gothic? Can't stories just work because of the content being all scary and stuff?"

"Excellent question, Liane," I said. "What do you think?"

"Well, I didn't sleep for two weeks after watching *Blair Witch*," Liane said. "And I didn't know anything about Gothic then. So I think stories can be effective either way. But knowing the conventions helps you talk about them differently or something, which is cool."

The sudden widespread reaching for backpacks indicated we'd reached the end of our class period.

"That's it for today, everyone."

I began gathering my own materials and putting them into my satchel.

"Dr. Maclean?" Fiona stood before me, an uncertain expression on her face.

"Yes?" I paused and smiled at her encouragingly.

"Some of us in the Literature Club wondered if you were available to help us."

"There's a literary club? I haven't heard about that yet."

"Yes, it's only a few years old, but some lit majors formed it so we could talk about the things we were reading in our classes. It started as a study group, actually." She paused before adding proudly, "I'm the president."

"Congratulations — that sounds fun."

"It's a blast," she said. "The school has an honor society chapter, of course, and most of us belong to that too, but not everyone can join the society since there's a grade point average requirement. Our club is open to all."

"That's nice. What do you need from me?"

"We need to think of a way to make money at Homecoming. The student organizations are allowed to have booths on Friday night at the football game, but we have to come up with a creative product to sell. We always try to do something related to literature because, well, that's the whole point." Fiona's hopeful expression won me over.

"Do you have an official faculty advisor?" I didn't want to step on anyone's toes.

"Professor James, but she's . . ."

"Not available," I hurried to complete the sentence. The last thing I wanted to do was discuss my jailed cousin with a student. "Do you have meetings, or how do you handle planning?"

"Meetings, mostly. Sometimes Dr. Hartwell comes too, but she's not usually involved."

"Well, if it's okay with the club, I'd be happy to help out."

Fiona said she would email me after talking to the rest of the members.

Back in the department, I knocked on Willa's door, which was partially open.

"Come in," she called. I pushed the door open and stepped inside, gasping a little at the vibrant tapestries in clashing designs covering every inch of the walls. There was something almost antagonistic about the visual effect here.

"Wow," I said, turning around in a full circle to take it all in. "There's so much to see."

"That's what everyone says. I know it's a bit much, but I like the contradictions of the dissimilar patterns."

"It's very . . . uh . . . vivid," I said. I was more of a minimalist, but to each her own.

She pointed to a chair in front of her desk. "Have a seat."

As I sat, she put down her pen and gave me her full attention.

"Fiona Graham asked me to help with the Literature Club booth for Homecoming while Calista is gone. I thought I'd check with you about it."

She smiled. "Thank you. I just asked Simone Raleigh to help out with the booth as well."

I registered a sinking feeling inside and rose to leave. "That's fine. I'll just tell Fiona you already have someone lined up —"

"Actually, Lila, we could use all the help we can get. Why don't you and Simone work together on this one?"

Willa didn't know that Simone was shaping up to be my archenemy, and I wasn't about to explain it to her. "You know, I'm a bit swamped, being new and all. So if you and Simone are already working on it —"

"We do need you. And it would be good service. Do you have anything in that column for your reappointment dossier yet?"

"No," I said. Definitely needed some service. "I'll do it, thanks."

"I'll give Simone your number, and you two can touch base."

"Okay," I said, trying to infuse my response with some enthusiasm.

She pulled open her desk drawer and extracted a file folder. "Before you go, let me give you more information about the club." She handed me a few stapled pages and slapped the folder shut. As she held the folder vertically and tapped it on her desk, I caught sight of what looked like a square of thorny branches penciled on the back of the folder.

"What's that?" I asked, pointing at it.

She turned the folder around and gave it a quick glance. Something in her face changed but I couldn't interpret her expression.

"A doodle, I guess," she said. "One of the students in the club — I don't know which one — put the folder in my mailbox so we could digitize the forms last year. I only have a few paper copies left, actually."

"The detective showed me a book with a similar symbol," I pressed, hoping she'd be the one to finally explain everything to me.

"Really?" She examined it again. "How odd."

She set the folder down on the desk while I debated whether or not to mention it had also been found on the knife. I decided to err on the side of caution — after all, my cousin was sitting in jail right now — and said nothing further.

"I'll be in touch, okay, Lila?" She smiled at me, then picked up her pen and started writing.

Our conversation appeared to be over.

As I walked home, I pondered the symbol.

Why did I keep seeing it? The folder didn't have a rose, but the thorns surely weren't coincidental. Or were they?

It hadn't even occurred to me that there might be students involved in anything as extreme as murder. I hoped not. But you never know. Maybe all of them were involved. Or perhaps some of them were involved but the others didn't know about it.

There was only one thing to do: infiltrate the Literature Club and figure it out for myself. It was sort of like going undercover, though my identity was already known and I was coming in as an advisory figure. Okay, so it was nothing like going undercover. But it was necessary. I ran through the plan in my mind.

Step One: Volunteer — or agree when forced — to help out with the Homecoming event.

Step Two: Meet with students to learn what said event involves.

Step Three: Gather evidence, obviously.

Step Four: Identify guilty parties, make Stonedale safe for all.

That could work if the murderers were, in fact, part of the group. Unless the murderers set their sights on me.

161

■ ■ ■ ■

"So what should we do for Homecoming? We have less than a month, so it can't be too complicated." Fiona addressed me expectantly the next day. We were in my office with Alex and Liane, who were also members of the Literature Club. Simone had texted that she was running late. I doubted she'd show up at all until we'd completed the work. Which was, I suspected, her plan in the first place. "But it has to be good so we can earn enough money to go to the Modern Language Association conference."

"You're going to MLA?" I asked, surprised. The annual conference was the event of the year for those involved in literature study. Scholars came from all over the world to present on panels, literary societies held meetings of various types, and many schools interviewed potential hires there too. Graduate students often attended, but it wasn't quite as typical for undergrads to go. Now I was even more impressed with their dedication to literature than I had been before, if that was possible.

"We've been attending the regional one, the Rocky Mountain MLA, which is awesome. But this year, we wanted to try to go to national. It's super expensive though," Fiona explained.

"Do you get any support from the university for that?" Calista had mentioned in passing that she'd attended a funding meeting a few weeks ago, though she hadn't said what it was for, specifically. I'd assumed it was for Gender Studies, but perhaps it was for the Literature Club.

Alex nodded briskly. "We do get some money, but it doesn't cover all of the expenses, so we need to subsidize it with whatever we can earn."

"What's the usual process?" I asked.

"We sell books that are donated by professors over the year. That usually nets us a few hundred. But that's not enough, so we have to do something else. Last year, we had a bake sale," said Liane, pushing her black glasses up on her nose. Her long blonde hair had been tipped in red in the trendy ombre style, which suited her.

"Yeah, but we only made seventy bucks from that," said Alex, sounding disgusted. He pulled off his cap and threw it on the floor next to his backpack. "We need much more than that."

"What else could we sell, aside from the books?" Liane asked. "And remember, we have to make whatever it is."

"What if we put literary quotes into fortune cookies this year?" Fiona mused while sketching a flower on her notepad.

"That's an interesting idea," I said encouragingly.

Alex shook his head. "That's even more work . . . and we'd probably make less money. Who buys a fortune cookie for a snack? At least the brownies sold well."

"Well, you come up with something, then," Fiona said, straightening up in her chair to give him a glare. "Don't be a hater."

Alex looked abashed momentarily, then cheered up. "What if we invested in some t-shirts and printed short quotes on them? I know a guy who silk screens. He has his own store and will give us a deal, I think. Plus, he'll make them fast." His voice grew stronger as he warmed to his topic. "We could do Bukowski and Kerouac —"

"And Toni Morrison and Jane Austen." Liane smiled at him.

The three of them began chattering excitedly. Before too long, they had divided up the duties and were texting other members of the Literature Club to distribute the work.

"What about copyright or trademarks, or whatever is appropriate if we're going to sell something?" I asked.

"I'll check into that," said Alex. "My friend who will do the silk screening knows all about that stuff because it's how he makes a living. He has a store."

"Thank you so much, Dr. Maclean," Fiona said, smiling shyly at me.

"You three did all the work," I said.

"But we appreciate your help," she added. "Really."

As I was about to broach the topic of the doodle on the folder, Simone swept into the room in an emerald-colored suit and a heady cloud of expensive perfume. "Oh, I'm so sorry," she said to the students. "I was caught up in a meeting with the chancellor. He's a dear friend of my mother's, and he invited me to lunch to see how the semester was going so far and, well, one doesn't run out on *him.*" She smiled warmly at them. They all smiled back and left.

Simone marched farther into my office and settled on my desk chair, placing her Birkin bag carefully on her lap. I sank reluctantly into the nearest seat just vacated by the students.

"How was the meeting?" she asked.

"It went well," I said. "They want to make t-shirts with literary quotes on them to sell at the Homecoming booth."

"Oh," she said, her nose wrinkling as if she had just caught a whiff of something offensive. "Do you think that's a good idea?"

"I do, actually. The students were excited about it as well."

"Was it your idea, Lila?" The question was presented with discernible disapproval.

"No — they came up with it themselves. But I think literary quotes are a superb thing to put on a shirt."

"I don't know that it's very appropriate."

"Appropriate?"

"You know, Stonedale has its standards, Lila."

"What do you mean by that?"

She lifted her chin. "I mean that it's not like every other school. It's special."

"Every school thinks it's special, Simone."

"But every school isn't, of course." She carefully smoothed the material of her skirt as she spoke. "This school caters to a certain kind of student. We need to be aware of their needs too."

"You're going to have to be more specific."

"See that's just it, Lila. If you belonged here, I wouldn't have to be." A sly look crossed her face. "You might also be interested to know I had a long chat with the chancellor about you and your cousin today. He was quite interested."

"What are you talking about?"

"Your cousin, the *murderer,*" Simone spit out, her eyes narrowed.

A rush of fury clenched my fists and rocketed up my volume. "She didn't kill anyone."

"Of course you'd say that. But it was her knife in his chest, was it not? Or perhaps we should talk about how you were the one who 'found' " — she leaned on the word heavily to emphasize her disbelief — "Roland dead. Perhaps it's a family business."

It took effort to speak calmly again, but I knew she loved seeing that she was getting to me, and I wanted to erase that satisfaction. "That's ridiculous. She's innocent. And so am I."

Simone's smile was bright and hard. "The chancellor isn't so sure. He was also very interested in hearing about your mother's . . . work."

I shrugged. "Great. It's art."

She tittered. "Not quite the type of art that this community endorses, on the whole."

"I thought you were just hired too. What makes you an expert on all things Stonedale?"

"Again, Lila, none of this should need explaining."

167

"Oh, please do enlighten me, Simone," I said, not bothering to temper the sarcasm in my voice.

"No, I don't think I will," she said, patting her pearls. "But rest assured that you won't last the semester."

CHAPTER 12

I pondered Simone's threat as I walked across campus a short while later. It was dusk, that magically gray time of day when things are less sharply defined. It suited my state of mind. Although I would never admit it out loud, she had scared me. I didn't know why she seemed to dislike me so much, unless it really was about my mother's art. That in and of itself did threaten some people.

Or perhaps it simply was about class, which Simone had all but stated outright. It was true that Calista and I didn't have privileged backgrounds like many of the faculty here — or the students, for that matter — but it was the twenty-first century, for goodness sakes.

Even if Simone were friends with the chancellor, could she have me fired? Wouldn't it take more than that? I sighed. I didn't know how it worked. Where there was a will, there was a way, so I couldn't ignore her completely. However, I'd be darned if I'd let her walk all over me.

Thus resolved, I strode a bit more briskly through the campus gates. I had a lot of grading to do tonight, and I wanted to get started. I sorted mentally through the dinner options waiting at home — yogurt or crackers and a lump of questionable cheddar cheese. I veered onto University Boulevard and walked a few blocks until I reached Scarlett's Café, vowing to restock my fridge at the earliest opportunity.

The bells on the door jingled as I entered the warm environment smelling of fresh bread, which was a very welcome contrast to the chilly evening. When the sun goes down in Colorado, it grows cold fast. I placed my order for soup and salad at the to-go counter and gratefully took the last available seat on one of the nearby wooden benches. I let the various sounds of voices wash over me for a few peaceful minutes.

"Lila, what a nice surprise. Are you here for dinner?" Judith stood before me in a camel-colored wool coat, with a red scarf draped beautifully in some incomprehensibly complex manner around her shoulders and neck.

"Just picking something up."

I waved at the to-go counter.

Judith looked over my head. "I'm expecting Willa. We meet once a month to talk about our research." I heard my name called from the counter, but Judith was still talking. "Would you like to join us? We could use an Americanist in the mix."

"I'd love to, another time, but I have grading to do tonight." The man at the counter yelled my name slightly louder. I cringed and pointed at him. "I think that's me, in fact."

"Oh yes, please go," said Judith, moving to her left so I could make my way back to the counter. When I returned, brown paper bag in hand, she was chatting with Willa, whose lilac jacket stood out among the sea of dark coats.

". . . it just started," Willa was saying. "Which will make the hike this weekend that much harder."

"Willa does fourteeners," Judith told me. "She's a marvelous athlete."

"More like someone who is unwilling to let the mountains beat me. I'm more determined than athletic, I think." Willa unbuttoned her jacket. "Hi, Lila. Everything go okay with the Lit Club?"

"Yes," I said.

"Glad to hear it. Thanks so much. Especially since . . ." Her hazel eyes held my gaze. "The Roland experience must have been tough."

"Judith was there too," I said quickly.

She smiled at Judith. "Yes, and we've already talked about it, but I haven't had a chance to check in with you. Sorry — too much going on, and I'm knackered. Oh, and poor Calista. How is she?"

We pooled our information on Calista and discovered that none of us knew much of anything yet. They asked several questions about her well-being and said they planned to visit her this week. Both told me to call upon them if they could be helpful to my cousin in any way. It was heartening to see how concerned they both were — which also provided some support for Calista's own faith in these two women. She always dismissed out of hand any suggestion I made about their possible involvement in the attacks of late.

I asked if they were on the tenure committee, hoping they'd have insight into the infamous Roland letter, but neither had heard any specifics about the contents.

Willa turned back to Judith. "In the meantime, Spencer just added me to the hiring committee to replace Roland."

"I'm on it too," said Judith.

Willa smiled. "I was hoping you were."

"Who are the other members?" Judith asked.

Willa performed a visual check of the room — front, back, and sides — until she was satisfied that we could speak freely. "The only one I'm bothered about is Norton. He's definitely on the list, for some reason I do not comprehend." Willa glanced at me. "Just between us, okay, Lila?"

"Sure." My ears pricked up. I was glad she appeared to trust me.

"Norton simply doesn't want the same things most of us seek. I'm certain he hopes to hire that horrid Eldon in Roland's place, which I think would be very unfortunate for our students. On a related note, I'm positive Norton will nominate himself for department chair again when that election comes around —"

"He's run countless times," Judith informed me. "Never wins."

Willa laughed. "Can you imagine if that daft twit was steering our department? We'd be utterly doomed."

Judith leaned her head closer to Willa's. "Not to dissuade you from your views, dear, but may I, with all love and support, suggest a more measured expression of them in public, perhaps?"

"Sorry. You're right," Willa said, appearing both impatient and chastened somehow. She started to poke around in the large leather crossbody bag she wore, then paused and covered her lips with her hand as she thought. "I can't remember who else is on the hiring committee, and I don't think I brought the list with me."

"What about Simone?" I asked, taking the chance to bring her name up. Although I'd just vowed not to let her govern my experience here at Stonedale, I needed to find out why she was so hostile.

"No," said Judith.

"Why do you ask?" Willa added.

"I don't know," I admitted. "She's on my mind, I guess." I flailed for words, knowing it wasn't prudent to gossip about fellow newbies in front of other faculty members, however delicately.

I decided to test the waters. "Simone seems very, uh, committed to the university," I said carefully.

"Her mother used to teach in the education department here, which may contribute to that," said Judith. "She was very proud of Stonedale."

"I could see how that would affect Simone's perspective," I said, trying to find the words to bring up her behavior. "We haven't had a chance to get to know each other yet, and she's been . . ."

"Unfriendly?" Willa asked.

Now or never, I guess. "Yes," I said firmly. "I don't know why. Maybe our personalities don't mesh or something."

"Well, I know why," said Willa.

Judith seemed surprised. "You do?"

"Indeed. It's like this, Lila. Her sister Selene interviewed for your job and didn't get it. You were hired instead. You are, *ipso facto,* an enemy."

I nodded but didn't say anything. What was there to say?

Judith gave Willa a reproachful look and put her arm on my shoulder. "Lila dear," she said, "I'm not sure it's as simple as that —"

"Oh, it's absolutely as simple as that," said Willa grimly. "I'm her faculty mentor, remember? We went out to dinner the other night. Simone couldn't have been less subtle about her innuendos where Lila was concerned. I'm not going to go into detail, but it's all rubbish. Not your fault, Lila. Not at all. Besides, Selene wasn't even an Americanist. I don't know why she was interviewed."

"Didn't she write her dissertation on Robert Frost?" Judith asked.

"John Donne, mostly, with gestures made to other authors," Willa said. "She'd clearly exaggerated the amount of attention paid to Frost in order to apply for the position, but from some of the comments she made, I didn't find the depth of her commitment to American literature to be persuasive. In any case, Simone shouldn't blame Lila for being a better candidate."

Judith appeared distressed, but her tone was calm and comforting. "Perhaps we could sort through this, the four of us?"

"I don't know," I said. Seemed pretty straightforward to me. Simone wanted me fired so she could try to get Selene hired. Or maybe Simone just wanted to punish me for landing the job over her sister. "Do you think it's necessary for us to talk about it? I wouldn't even know what to say."

"Maybe not," said Willa. "You and Simone working on the Literature Club together might alleviate some of the tension, just as a natural result. That's one reason I urged you to do it, by the way."

"Oh," I said.

"Yes, and thank you for taking that work on, Lila," said Judith. "It's so important to the students." She smiled at me.

"Just don't let Simone get to you," advised

Willa, in her blunt but not unkind way.
Easier said than done.

CHAPTER 13

This month's mentoring meeting was focused on the expectations for tenure-track faculty. Stonedale's motto, "Ever More," was certainly appropriate, I thought, studying the large framed school crest on the wall behind Chancellor Wellington, who seemed positively giddy as he reeled off the achievements for which we would need to strive: the highest possible course evaluations, to be supported by the highest possible faculty observation reports, with the highest possible student advising numbers and membership on the highest possible number of committees — divided among department, college, and university — plus, of course, a book or two. "With," he added, flashing a smile, "the best possible press."

I'm sure I wasn't the only one in the room who was having difficulty breathing at the thought that we were supposed to accomplish the best possible everything, which meant that excelling was the lowest possible standard, but I was the only one who found herself horrified to have raised her hand. The chancellor gently flicked a piece of lint from the arm of his immaculate suit, which no doubt cost more than my whole monthly — maybe yearly — salary, and nodded at me.

"Thank you for that explanation, Chancellor Wellington. May I ask a question?"

He waved his hand benevolently to indicate that I should speak.

"Is there a certain number in each category for which we should aim?"

Chancellor Wellington leaned back in his chair and crossed his arms. "Mentors? Would you like to answer this one?" It was impossible to tell if he didn't know the answer or if he was simply disinclined to provide a concrete standard — in other words, something tangible for which to aim. That is not how academia works, generally speaking. For example, with your doctoral dissertation, you must go boldly where no scholar has gone before; however, you must also choose something that allows your claims to be supported by existing research, which narrows down the whole originality aspect quite a bit. Moreover, you need to choose something familiar enough that your committee members can remain the experts during the process, which eliminates pretty much anything they have not read. I'd somehow muddled through that project, but now that my career was on the line, I was desperate for clarity.

Judith turned to me. "There isn't one number per se, Lila. But there is a picture, developed over time, created by the annual evaluations performed by the chair, in which each of the areas is addressed —"

She was interrupted by an irritated-looking professor whose table card identified him as being from Political Science. "We rank you. Annually," he snapped. As if Judith hadn't just said that.

Simone regarded him delightedly, clearly enjoying his contribution to my mortification.

"But how do we know if we're on track to meeting the annual requirements?" I asked, noting relief cross the faces of several other new professors — they may have had the same question, or perhaps they were just glad they weren't the one blurting things out, as I seemed unable to stop myself from doing.

Irritated Prof sighed deeply and drummed his fingers on the table. Chancellor Wellington smoothed his silk tie while glaring at

Judith, silently demanding she shut me up.

But she didn't, bless her heart. Instead, she asked if anyone else wanted to talk about annual evaluations. After a silent pause, a few hands went up. Then a few more. She smiled sweetly at the chancellor. "Do you think it might be useful to spend a moment on the reappointment process?"

The chancellor, seizing the chance to seem magnanimous, nodded regally. "Indeed. Why don't you give a brief overview, Dr. Westerly?"

As we walked out of the meeting, Judith squeezed my arm. "Don't worry, Lila. You weren't the only one to have questions. Keep asking when something is unclear."

I knew I was lucky to have an actual mentor in Judith, not just a faculty member going through the motions.

"I'm here for you, Lila," Judith continued. "Do you have any other concerns?"

"Only that I won't be able to publish anything on time or in the right places. Roland seemed very doubtful about my topic."

"There's a reason 'publish or perish' is whispered in the shadowy groves of academia — it can be a dangerous place. People disappear every year."

If this was her idea of a pep talk, it wasn't

helping. Not one bit.

"However, this does not mean *you* are destined to disappear." Judith tucked a lock of long white hair behind her ear and lowered her voice. "Yes, you have to publish scholarship — we all do — but rest assured that most people don't accomplish much research the first semester, or even during the first year in many cases. Rational people know it takes a while to sort through the demands of the position. Others, however, feel it their duty to keep the pressure on new hires. Roland was the latter type: he knew asking about it would upset you, so he did."

I managed a small nod.

"I'm telling you how it is. Not how it should be." She punctuated this by leaning forward to bestow a quick hug, whereby I was briefly smothered by the abundant fringe of her scarf and a burst of lavender scent. "In such situations, one simply does what one can."

Whatever that meant. "Thanks, Judith. I'm sorry I brought it up. It doesn't matter."

"But it does matter. Please don't apologize, dear."

"Jude!" A petite woman with spiky white hair strode up and hugged Judith. She wore an embroidered tunic and denim skirt with ornate cowboy boots. There was a palpable sense of energetic purpose emanating from her, as if she were on the way to some magnificent adventure.

I took a step backwards, then remained uncomfortably right where I was — torn between giving them space and waiting to speak more with Judith.

"I only have a second," the woman warned Judith. "I'm racing to meet my sister, and you know how she is about being on time." They laughed lightly, as if it were a recurring refrain.

Judith beckoned me over. "Lila, I'm so pleased to introduce you to one of my dearest friends, Elisabetta Vega. Liz, meet Lila Maclean, who took over your position."

Elisabetta beamed as she thrust out her hand to shake mine. "So you're the new me — how do you like it here so far?"

There was something welcoming about her, as if we'd been friends for years — probably the reason I said it was "a bit scary" instead of something more formal and appropriate for a new professor. She chuckled.

Judith moved closer to us and lowered her voice. "Liz, have you heard about Roland?"

Elisabetta's grin disappeared. "Tragic."

I spoke quietly. "You were all close friends, weren't you? I'm sorry for your loss."

They shared a look that seemed laden with meaning but was impenetrable, then murmured their thanks.

Judith snapped her fingers. "I want to tell you before I forget — the emeritus vote has been pushed back until further notice, given the circumstances." She looked at me and explained, "Liz is up for professor emerita this year."

I congratulated Elisabetta.

She gave me a warm smile. "I have an idea — why don't we three have dinner sometime soon?"

We made arrangements to meet next week, and I went back to my office. I stuffed my laptop into my bag along with papers that needed to be graded and walked through the empty department until I reached the main office. It was slightly after five, and I figured Millicent would still be there. She didn't seem like someone who shaved minutes off of the work day. The Literature Club had asked me to check on the status of the book stock — they were stored in the bowels of the building somewhere. It would give us all a chance to see what we were dealing with and how pressing the additional sales items would be, in terms of the students being able to hit their goal.

I greeted Millicent, who was making notations on something. Classical music was playing softly in the background. When she saw me, she put down the pen and waited for me to speak.

"Sorry to bother you, but I was wondering if you could please tell me where the books are stored when professors donate them for the Literature Club sale? I'm helping out this year."

"We keep those down in the basement," she said. "Some students bring them up right before the sale. We can't have them sitting around here all year in the meantime."

"I won't remove them," I assured her quickly. "We're just trying to get an idea of what's there."

Millicent reached into the side drawer and removed a box of keys with colored tags attached. "I'm about to leave for the night, but if you promise to return this promptly, I'll let you take it."

"Perfect, thanks," I said, waiting until she reached out to drop the key into my hand. The blue rectangular tag read "Storage Room 12."

"The door is marked. You shouldn't have

any trouble finding it." She picked up the pen and resumed her work.

I went down Crandall's side stairwell, whose utilitarian nature contrasted the marble steps leading to the classrooms in the main hall. The thick fire door at the bottom had been well-oiled — it opened noiselessly, and I found myself in a plain white, gently curving hallway. Closed wooden doors were evenly spaced out along the dimly lit, eerie corridor in front of me. I'd never been a fan of basements, always expecting something to jump out of the dark corners. I shivered and tried not to let my imagination get the best of me. It was at times like these that a steady diet of Gothic and mystery did not serve me so well.

Eventually, I saw the storage room sign. I was so far along that I wasn't sure I was even in Crandall anymore — I seemed to be heading to Randsworth Hall. I wondered if this passageway extended throughout campus, or just between certain buildings. Hadn't Nate mentioned something about underground tunnels at one point? I needed to check with him. The corridor hooked just past the storage door, and I couldn't see around it. I fitted the key into the lock. The sooner I got this over with, the better.

Inside, I felt along the wall until I located

a switch, which illuminated a single bulb dangling from the ceiling. Shelves lined the room, some draped with intricate spider webs. There didn't seem to be much rhyme or reason to the contents — a large collection of empty three-ring notebooks on one, an old mimeograph machine next to an adding machine on another, and stacks of files on the next. I spied books on the shelves at the far wall and headed towards them.

After a half hour of digging, I stood back and surveyed the lot, brushing my hands on the side of my pants to get rid of the dust. The students would be glad — there were at least two hundred books here. Some were in boxes and others were stacked haphazardly, but the pile included a number of textbooks, various guides to literary periods or theories, and many paperbacks: everything from classic novels to contemporary poetry to sci-fi. Looked like we were set for a sale.

I picked up my bag, turned off the bulb, and pulled the door shut behind me, noticing that there was light spilling into the hallway through the half-open door to the next room.

That light had *not* been on before.

Was someone else down here?

I knocked on the door, my heart beating faster. The knocks echoed, but there was no response, so I pushed on the wood and stepped inside. I expected to find myself in another rectangular storage room, but it was a large circular space, the center portion of which was about a foot lower than the rest and filled with folding chairs. A wooden podium against the far wall faced the rows of chairs. What was this room supposed to be? I couldn't imagine why anyone else would come down to this strange place unless they were up to no good. Which reminded me that someone had recently been killed in this very building. Definitely time to leave. I hurried across the room and flipped the light switch. Moving steadily along the corridor, I headed back the way I'd come, skirting the fine line between walking and running so as to cover the most ground while making the least amount of noise until I'd made it out of Crandall Hall altogether.

Through the walk home, the long soak in a hot tub, the sleepless night, and the entire day that followed, I pondered why somebody might be lurking down there without saying anything.

And came to no conclusions whatsoever.

CHAPTER 14

On Monday afternoon, I met with the Lit Club students in my office to go over the details for Homecoming. Alex's friend had come through as promised, and the shirts were ready.

"You were right," said Alex, as he held up a green cotton t-shirt. "The rules around quotations are mega-complicated. Parody, however, is given much more leeway. So I went with something from Alexander Pope's 'Essay on Criticism' but tweaked it for our purposes."

"These are amazing," I said, examining the words in a large stylized font proclaiming, "To err is human / To read, divine." Beneath, in smaller capital letters, was the name of the club. Alex handed shirts to Fiona and Liane. The other students and I gushed for a few minutes. Alex usually had a serious expression, but in response to the praise, his whole face lit up.

"I think I like these even better than reproducing other people's quotes, Alex. I'd like to buy one right now. How much are they?"

"You can have one, Dr. Maclean," he said with a grin. "For helping us. And please take one for Professor James as well."

"That's so kind, thank you." I selected a bright red one for Calista and a magenta one for myself. "But since this is a fundraising effort, I'd like to pay for them both."

"We don't have the box ready yet," said Fiona, as she carefully folded her yellow shirt into a neat square and placed it on top of her backpack.

"What box?" I asked.

"We have to withdraw money from our club bank account so we can make change. Then we keep it in a lockbox. It should be down in the basement with the books. Professor James usually gets it for us the week of the sale."

"Okay," I said. "Let's ask Dr. Raleigh to be the box person this year since she wants to help out." And since she hasn't done anything else to be of service, I thought but didn't say. "So who will do that?"

Liane raised her hand as if we were in class. "I'm the treasurer, so I'll do it."

"How many officers are there?" I asked,

realizing I didn't know.

"Four," said Alex. "Liane's the treasurer, as she just said. I'm the VP, Fiona's the president, and Carter is the PR guy."

"I haven't met Carter," I said.

"He's, like, a text-only person," said Liane solemnly. "Tries not to leave his dorm room."

"Gamer," added Alex.

"He keeps our Facebook page and Twitter updated," added Fiona. "He's glued to his computer most of the time. We just fill him in after meetings and he advertises whatever we need through social media."

"Okay. Do you need anything else from me right now?"

"No," she said. "I think we're good."

We spent some time talking about the cost to make the shirts versus the amount the students needed to earn and came up with a price to charge.

"We should all wear these ahead of time to stir up some buzz," Alex said, indicating his own dark blue shirt. "What do you think?"

"Totally agree," said Fiona. "I'll wear mine tomorrow."

"Me too," added Liane. She gazed happily at the peach-colored shirt on her lap. "I love it."

"Wear them as much as you can," said Alex.

"Great work, everyone." As they began packing up, I asked them to take a look at a piece of paper on which I'd sketched the thorn-and-rose design. I watched closely as they passed it around, but they seemed unfamiliar with the symbol.

"What is that?" asked Fiona.

"Just something a friend showed me," I said. "We don't know what it means. It was on the back of a folder. Any ideas?"

None of them recognized it or even seemed very interested in it.

"Let me ask you this: how well did you know Dr. Higgins?"

Liane grimaced. "He was my Brit Lit survey professor. Super strict. He could be rude too. But I learned a lot." She paused for a moment. "Really sad, what happened to him, though."

"It is," I said. "Did you know anyone who might have wanted him, uh, gone?"

They didn't have any theories about that and soon went back to zipping their backpacks and chatting. So much for my information-gathering plan.

Simone drifted in, making a big performance of checking her watch several times. "I was sure we were meeting at four. Is my watch slow? How long have you been here?" She fluttered around a bit apologizing, then we spent about ten minutes bringing her up to speed on all of the details. She was extremely complimentary about the shirts, though, and the students seemed pleased with her response. So at least she did that.

An hour later, the late afternoon sunlight shining through the yellow leaves outside my window cast a golden aura over everything in the office. While breathtaking, it made me long for the spectacular reds that were a hallmark of east coast autumns. I allowed myself precisely one minute of nostalgia before returning my attention to the tedious task of proofreading an exam I was giving my American Lit class this week.

I gathered up my things and went to drop off the exam, which couldn't be copied by student workers so as to protect the integrity of the test. I had to give it to Millicent, who had already made it clear she hated copying exams, so I approached the task with a small amount of dread. She'd been fine the last time we spoke, but you never know.

Her desk was empty, but Roland's — now Eldon's — office door was open and the lights were on. I took a few steps forward and called her name, dropping my bag next to her desk. I peeked inside Eldon's office and did a quick visual sweep, but it was empty. She wasn't here, and I was going to have to sit here and wait.

Or I could make better use of my time.

I went back to the hallway and checked to be sure no one was coming, then ran over to the row of filing cabinets across from Millicent's desk. I yanked open the top drawer of the closest one to look for a folder of tenure letters. I knew it was a long shot, but if I could at least see what Roland's letter said, I might be able to help my cousin's defense.

Nothing relevant there. I repeated my search in all four drawers of all five cabinets, but I couldn't find anything with "tenure" or her name on it. They must keep sensitive personnel files locked up somewhere else. I pushed the final drawer closed and stood up.

As I paused to stretch my aching back, my eyes caught on a stack of manila folders resting on the surface of the cabinets. The highest folder was so full that the cover was angled slightly up, revealing the word "Mysteries" in large black markered letters across the front.

I stared at it. It must be my course proposal. But why was it so thick? My proposal had only been five pages long. Perhaps the folder contained comments from the curriculum committee meeting. Those would be very useful to see since I planned to revise and resubmit now that Roland was no longer in charge.

I reached out my hand, hesitating with my palm hovering over the cover. Surely a quick peek wouldn't hurt anything.

Just this once.

Especially if no one saw me do it.

Flipping the cover open quickly, I noted several stapled packets inside. However, these had nothing to do with my course proposal. The top one was an essay, in manuscript form, on an author I had never heard of named Eve Turner. I slid it aside and thumbed through the rest of the stack. The remaining packets were articles that had been published in various journals. Each piece was on a different author and genre — everything from thriller to cozy — but written by the same person, Poe Collins. Unquestionably a pseudonym — it was hard to miss the combination of two writers who had been called "fathers" of the mystery genre in one way or another: Edgar Allan and Wilkie. There were no additional papers inside, so I closed the folder and darted over to the visitor chair.

I settled in to wait, and as the minutes continued to tick by, I wondered who the other mystery scholar in the department might be — clearly, someone was using the literary criticism of "Poe Collins" for something. I hadn't run across that name while writing my dissertation, but that didn't mean much. There is a veritable sea of scholarship through which one must wade for any given topic, and staying focused is necessary. In fact, sometimes it's the only thing that keeps us afloat.

I couldn't ask Millicent who it was, either, given that I'd only discovered the information while snooping. I continued to turn the discovery over in my mind. The longer I sat there, the more I was surrounded by the intoxicating fragrance of the bouquet of mixed flowers — lilies, tulips, daisies, and some spiky things I didn't recognize — next to Millicent's computer. I leaned over, close enough to breathe in the scent even more, inadvertently hitting the tallest bloom with my chin. A white card fell onto the desk: "All my love, B." I picked it up and studied the handwriting. Could B stand for Bartholomew? Spencer was one of the few professors Millicent seemed to like. Maybe the only one, now that Roland was gone. Of course, it could be someone else altogether, someone non-English-department-related.

As I tried to poke the card back into the arrangement, I heard Millicent clear her throat. I twisted around in my seat, still holding the card, which I held out silently.

"Nosy, are we?"

She walked around her chair, set down a paperback book, and reached across the desktop to snatch the card from me. It went into her capacious side drawer, which she slammed shut. After plunking down in her chair, she yanked at the hem of her beige polyester suit.

"I'm sorry, Millicent. I didn't mean to see your card. I was just trying to smell the flowers —"

"What can I do for you, Lila?" Apparently, we weren't going to discuss it.

"What are you reading? I'm always looking for recommendations." I pointed to the paperback she'd just placed on the desk. The cover was facing down, so I angled my head to try and read the spine. Couldn't help myself.

She slowly moved her elbow sideways so that it was positioned in front of the book.

I switched gears. Maybe she was a mystery fan. Maybe we could bond a little bit. Maybe she would explain what that folder meant. "What's your favorite genre?"

"I'll read anything," she said flatly.

"What's that one?" I pointed again at the paperback. She didn't respond.

We stared at each other like two boxers waiting for the bell to ring.

Eventually, Millicent sighed, slid the book closer, and flipped it over. A muscled hottie whose unbuttoned shirt was rippling in the wind clasped a long-haired beauty in a corset.

"Romance?" I tried to hide my surprise. Never would have guessed. "Well, if you come across anything great . . ." My hand circled to indicate potential sharing of information, and I smiled at her.

She did not smile back. I was sure no recommendations would be coming my way any time soon.

"Do you usually buy books at the Literature Club sale?"

"Yes. I try to support the students whenever possible."

"Looks as though there will be a lot to choose from this year. I saw at least two hundred books down in the basement. Which reminds me, I still have the key." I pulled it out of my bag and returned it to her. "What is the big room in the basement used for?"

"The department doesn't use anything

besides storage space in the basement. Why?"

"There was a light on in the room next door, so I peeked inside. It's a huge circular room, and there were chairs set up, so I thought perhaps someone was having a meeting."

Millicent shrugged. "A janitor must have left it on. No one holds meetings down there."

She was probably right.

I explained the exam issue. She informed me that it would be available Wednesday morning in a tone that conveyed irritation and indifference in equal amounts.

That evening, after fixing myself a cup of peppermint tea, I settled in to do some class preparation. Despite the real-life drama demanding my attention, classes marched ever onward. I sat down at my kitchen table with the books I'd need to catch up. The American Lit survey covered everything since 1865 and progressed necessarily at the speed of light. I had the sneaking suspicion I'd assigned far too much reading. It would probably take a few semesters to calibrate the pace of the class. In the meantime, I would just have to scramble. But first I'd prepare Gothic, which for me was the literary equivalent of having my dessert first.

I cracked open the cover of the thick anthology but, after fifteen minutes of reading the same page over again and still not knowing what it said, I found myself staring out the window, thinking about today's class meeting on Charlotte Perkins Gilman's story, "The Yellow Wallpaper." Gilman's tale always prompted energetic discussion — the narrator's relentless journaling of her descent into a dark state of obsession is gripping indeed.

After discussing the text at length as an example of psychological realism, describing a woman suffering from depression, I asked them to see if they could make an argument for the events being, instead, supernaturally charged experiences. I'd heard multiple gasps as students, upon a second reading, saw that the same symbols and elements could be read in multiple ways. It helped when they noticed that the narrator says upfront she hopes the house will be haunted.

The mysterious rose symbol popped into my mind. What did it mean? It was all well and good to compare realistic and Gothic readings when connected to a text, but not quite as comfortable in reality. Whenever I mentioned the symbol — or whatever it was — no one offered any explanation, but then another one appeared. What was the connection to the attacks? Was I imagining some kind of ominous conspiracy where there wasn't any? The only thing I knew for certain was Detective Archer had found the symbol interesting enough to mention.

Getting nowhere with my reading, I pulled out a folder of papers that needed attention. Trying to catch up on grading was a Sisyphean task: as soon as I completed one stack of papers, another one rolled in. But that never stopped me from believing I could carve out a little reprieve somehow. And so it goes.

When my phone trilled and my mother's name popped up on the screen, I gladly set down my pen and answered. I'd brought her up to speed a few days ago, and she'd been sending supportive texts around the clock.

"How's Calista doing?"

"I don't know. She's . . . not herself."

"That's to be expected. By the way, I've hired a new lawyer for her. Don't let Calista fire her. She'll say it's too expensive and she'll figure something out herself, but this is my niece we're talking about. I'm not going to leave it up to chance. Anyway, Tara

— that's her name — probably has seen Calista by now."

A rush of relief ran through me. "Thanks so much. I was worried about that."

"Now, on to you," she said briskly, as if she were running down a checklist in front of her. "Are you okay?"

"Technically. I mean, I'm functioning. It's just . . . horrible."

"I know," she said. "But you have to stay strong. And do everything you can to help her."

"I am," I said, though my mom had already accomplished more than I had on that front, from New York to boot. She was efficient that way.

"Give Calista my love, darling, and tell her I'm making plans to come to Stonedale at the earliest possible moment," she added. "I have a deadline coming up on some commissioned work to go in front of a new office building. One of those developer deals where they want a sculpture to go along with whatever they're naming the place. You know how difficult it is for me to try and be creative within someone else's parameters, and I'm really struggling, or I'd be out there already."

"I hope it doesn't come to a trial." It was surreal to imagine my cousin in that situation. Didn't even seem possible that she was a suspect in the first place, much less a defendant.

"If it does, we'll just have to do our best. Didn't someone famous say that?"

"I don't know," I said. "But they were right."

CHAPTER 15

I hurried to the café where I was meeting Judith and Elisabetta for dinner, trying to decide if I should bring up the thorn-and-rose design. I suspected it would make me sound crazy, but I didn't have anyone else to ask. Judith had already told me she didn't know what it meant when we'd discussed the book, so that was probably a dead end anyway. Still. Perhaps I should just go with the conversation, and if it felt right at some point to toss a query onto the table, I'd do it. I entered the front door into the warm, fragrant restaurant and saw the women sitting in a booth in front of the fireplace. They both smiled and waved me over.

"So glad you could make it," said Judith, patting the spot next to her. She was wearing a brocade jacket with another one of her amazing scarves arranged artfully over the top. Someday I would have to ask her to show me how she got them to defy gravity like that. My scarves always unwrapped themselves and slithered to the floor, flew off my shoulders as I walked, or otherwise tried to escape when I wasn't looking.

I slid onto the leather seat and settled in.

"Are you hungry? The food is fabulous here," Elisabetta said, handing me a menu.

We all read quietly for moment, then gave our selections to the waiter who appeared to materialize out of thin air at the right moment — sign of a good restaurant. Then I turned to Judith and asked how she was feeling.

"I'm fine, thanks. As I kept telling the nurses and doctors, it was nothing."

"Jude, it was not nothing — you were attacked in your own home," Elisabetta said. "I can't imagine who did this, but they deserve to be caught. And I hope they are prosecuted to within an inch of their lives."

"Can you think of anyone who might be upset with you?" I almost anticipated Judith would know exactly who it was — she seemed so in tune with everything that went on at Stonedale.

She winked at me. "Dear heart, we all make people angry at some point. It's part of life. I hope whoever it was has now gotten that out of their system and we can all move on. It doesn't do anyone a bit of good to live in fear."

Elisabetta made an exasperated sound.

I took a small bite of the green salad just set down by the waiter, whose name, he had reminded us for the twelfth time, was Franz. We promised to let Franz know if we needed anything else, and he melted away from the table.

After shaking pepper onto her salad, Elisabetta smiled at me. "Lila, I know we snapped you up right after you finished your Ph.D. However, I'm afraid I don't know much more than that, other than that you're an Americanist. What was your dissertation topic?"

"I wrote about a mystery writer named Isabella Dare."

Elisabetta put her fork down and leaned forward. "How wonderful. I'm a mystery lover too. Where did you hear about her?"

I repeated the story about having found the box with Dare's work at the used bookstore.

"Very interesting," said Elisabetta. "Tell us about them."

"They're mysteries at the core, and they not only situate themselves within the Gothic tradition in obvious ways, but also play with the conventions in order to subvert certain ideologies of the day."

"They sound fascinating," said Judith.

"Who was Isabella?" asked Elisabetta.

"She lived a quiet life in New York City. Didn't really mix with other writers, but it's obvious she read widely. My committee director believed the texts were important enough on their own to be dissertation-worthy. I was so relieved because I wasn't convinced I had anything new to say about my original topic, which was Sylvia Plath."

"Did you know my dissertation was on Plath?" Elisabetta leaned forward.

Now it was my turn to be intrigued. "I didn't. What was your focus?"

"Oh, it was very in keeping with the times: I argued for Plath's rightful place within the literary tradition . . . you know, something so obvious to us these days but back then, it had to be proven."

"That's what I hope to do for Isabella too," I said, then something clicked. "Wait, you're E. G. Vega? Your book about Plath is terrific. I'm embarrassed I didn't realize who you were before. I thought —"

"You thought E.G. was a man? That was the idea." Elisabetta smiled. "What can I say? I was full of fire and fury in those days. I half-hoped some pompous ass would make the mistake and write about me as male so I could correct him in public."

"You're still full of fire and fury, Liz," Judith said.

"Yes, but I've learned to tamp it down to a simmer for everyday living."

"You're splendid either way, dear friend," said Judith.

After a sip of delicious cabernet, I asked, "Did you two meet here at Stonedale?"

"Nope," said Elisabetta. "Cal."

"She means Berkeley," clarified Judith.

Elisabetta regarded her fondly. "We went through the Ph.D. program together, a bonding experience if there ever was one, as you know."

"How nice that you could work at the same school." I missed my own grad school friends, all of whom had relocated to wherever the job market took them: we were scattered all over America and beyond.

"Indeed. It's very rare that two people from the same college are hired on tenure track — at least close together. We still can't explain how that happened, one right after the other."

Judith held up her wine glass. "Ours is not to wonder why, right?" And with that, we all took a sip.

Franz appeared as if on cue, placing our plates gently before us and inquiring about any additional needs. He deserved a hefty tip.

We went about the business of eating, then Elisabetta asked if we'd heard anything about the Roland investigation. Judith and I both shook our heads. Recognizing a chance to ask some questions, I went for it.

"Were you all very close friends?"

"For a long time, we were," said Judith, regarding Elisabetta thoughtfully.

Elisabetta put down her fork. "Actually, three of us were. Jude and Spence were together, and I adored them, and Roland was Spencer's friend, so he was always hanging around."

"So you didn't adore him too?"

Elisabetta sighed. "No. Not at all. I tried to tolerate him, but it was uncomfortable."

"Why, if you don't mind me asking?"

"Lila, you met him, right?" Elisabetta asked, watching me closely.

"Yes."

"So you know he was an overbearing and outspoken man, with opinions that were not only antiquated but also hurtful. I arrived, focused completely on beginning this new career and he swooped in like a hawk and began ordering me around. And it had a strong romantic component, as if I were a mail-order bride. Just because Jude and

Spence had connected, he acted as though the universe had conjured me up as a mate for him. It was unbelievable."

"What happened?"

"Well, for one thing, he wouldn't leave me alone — always showing up at just the right moment when I had to walk across campus so he could accompany me. He brought me flowers and gifts all the time. I did not want them. He called me at home so often I had to quit answering the phone. He —" She stopped suddenly.

"May I?" Judith said, quietly.

Elisabetta nodded her assent.

"He couldn't believe Liz wasn't interested in him, so he orchestrated inappropriate touches — a brush here, a squeeze there — and joked far too often that she was 'just playing hard to get, as befits a lady.' "

I gaped at her.

"But that's sexual harassment."

"It is," said Elisabetta. "But, as a new faculty member, I didn't want to create a scandal. I needed this job. I'd seen what had happened to women in the profession before me who had dealt with similar situations. Also, I was involved with another professor and didn't want her to be subjected to the scrutiny that would follow. That bastard simply wasn't worth it."

"I understand why you would want to protect someone, but still, I can't believe you had to go through that."

"It's embarrassing to admit this, but I was just afraid. All of my bluster about being strong enough to handle it on my own was crap, and Nala knew it. She was very angry with me — she wanted me to take formal action, to make sure he was officially reprimanded. We fought about that for thirty years, actually, but I was stubborn. Not proud of that now. I wish I could tell her she was right."

"You're not together anymore?" I was horrified to see tears well up in Elisabetta's eyes.

Judith patted Elisabetta's arm while talking to me. "Nala passed away last year, Lila. She was sick for a long time."

"I'm so sorry, Elisabetta."

She struggled to regain her composure, then excused herself from the table.

"Oh, Judith, I'm sorry." Clearly Elisabetta was still suffering a great deal.

"It's not your fault, Lila. She's grieving."

I nodded.

"They were a perfectly matched couple — true soulmates — and they were very happy." She frowned slightly. "It's just unfortunate that they had to deal with Roland."

"So you were in the middle."

"Not really," she said. "Roland was always more Spence's friend than mine. Like Liz, I tolerated him for Spence's sake. But it was difficult. Once he found out about Nala, he did everything in his power to punish them both professionally. He argued against Liz's tenure bid and promotions, though she still received them. And Nala was a history professor who single-handedly brought about the existence of the African-American Studies department. Roland, of course, as a loud presence on the Faculty Senate, opposed it. It was an ugly, drawn-out battle. But Nala was a fighter, and she never let his idiocy slow her down. She just persevered."

"She sounds amazing."

"She was." Judith paused. "And Liz is deeply depressed about her death. I wish I could do more for her."

"I'm sure she appreciates your support," I tried to console her.

"All we can do is offer our condolences, I suppose, but I do feel rather helpless." I had never seen Judith uncertain before, and it was unnerving. I noticed the bill in its leather folder resting on the table, which Franz had invisibly produced for us somehow, and reached for it. "I'll pay for this."

I turned to rummage in my bag for my wallet, and my fingertips touched metal. The necklace.

She held out her hand. "No, Lila — I'd like to take care of it."

I gave Judith the bill, thanking her as I pulled out the chain.

Franz arrived to collect payment, giving me a moment to collect my thoughts. When he left, I gently set the necklace down on the table between us with the rose-and-thorn emblem facing up. "Have you ever seen this before?"

She gave me a brilliant smile. "Oh, it's lovely. Would you mind if I took a closer look?"

"Please do."

She examined it.

"It matches the symbol in the book used to . . ."

"Get me?" Judith sounded amused. "Yes, you mentioned that the book was embossed when you came to see me in the hospital, didn't you? It does sound like an unusual coincidence to see the same pattern on both."

Out of the corner of my eye, I saw Elisabetta approaching from across the room, so I spoke hurriedly. "Do you know what it means?"

Judith held the disk at arm's length. She frowned. "Sorry, I can't see details anymore without my glasses." She studied the symbol for what seemed like a long period of time, during which I wondered if she was thinking up a plausible explanation. But finally, she shrugged and put it down. "I can't help you, dear."

Well, that was incredibly unhelpful. Perhaps it was best to hold off on the whole rose-thingies-might-be-evil conversation for the time being.

When Elisabetta returned, Judith changed the subject to what we were currently reading. We spent another fifteen minutes or so talking about a bestselling mystery they'd both enjoyed. Elisabetta offered to loan me the book and suggested we swing by on our way home. We'd already discovered her house was only a few blocks from mine — one thing I loved about Stonedale was the ability to walk almost everywhere, even at night, thanks to Stonedale's dedication to street lights. They were designed in a quaint style to evoke an earlier era and placed all over the town. There must be a lamp post company somewhere that was very happy to have won the Stonedale contract.

We said goodbye to Judith and set out

along the sidewalks, past neat rows of bungalows and Victorians nestled side by side. I was glad we were together — the recent attacks were always on my mind as I walked around Stonedale at night. I wasn't willing to give up my freedom, but I had regular prickles of concern about my solo jaunts. Soon we reached Elisabetta's house, a large stone cottage with tall firs on either side of the front lawn. It would have made the perfect cover for a romantic suspense novel if it hadn't been tucked into a residential street but situated instead on a windswept moor.

After Elisabetta unlocked the door, we went inside. I stepped onto a long red floral runner that extended the length of the hallway. Mahogany banisters gleamed along the staircase to the left.

"This way, Lila," she said, moving to the right.

I followed her into a room with wall-to-wall bookcases and a black leather sectional flanked by a pair of reading lamps. A fleece blanket folded neatly over one corner of the sofa invited you to curl up beneath it immediately. It was a reader's dream.

She turned around, her finger on her lips, thinking. "You know, I believe it's upstairs on my nightstand. Make yourself comfortable while I go take a look."

I gladly moved closer to the bookshelves, which resembled mine with everything from classical Greek drama to contemporary fiction and poetry, and horizontal books placed on top of the vertical ones — in other words, stuffed into all available spaces. She also had several sections devoted to mysteries, which made me smile, and numerous stacks of books on the floor next to the shelves. I would have bet that her office had once contained hundreds more, as did mine. Occasionally I tried to streamline, but one never knew when it might be necessary to dig up the source of an allusion; thus, my efforts had so far been unsuccessful. I had just tilted my head to read the titles when one caught my eye.

It resembled the red volume that Detective Archer had shown me, though this one was called *Selected Works of Sylvia Plath*. I held the book flat on my right palm and opened the cover carefully with my left hand. As I began flipping toward the title page, I was half-hoping the symbol would be there and half-hoping it wouldn't. Even though I was prepared for it, my breath still caught in my throat at the sight of the rose and thorns embossed on the white stock.

Dang, they were everywhere.

When I heard footsteps coming down the stairs, I quickly set the book back on top of the stacks. But then I picked it up again. No time like the present.

Elisabetta walked up to me, smiling. "Found it."

I thanked her and held out the red book. "What's this one?"

Her smile faded briefly, then she rekindled the wattage.

"Oh, it's just a collection of Plath's work." She handed me the paperback and took the other one from me.

I pointed to the red volume, which she held next to her chest, arms crossed. I'd apparently have to wrestle her to get another chance at examining it.

"That one has a symbol embossed on the front page. What is that?"

She didn't move. "I don't know."

"Could I show you?"

Her arms remained crossed. "No, I've seen it, but I really couldn't say what it is."

"It's just that . . . well, it keeps showing up, including on the book that was used to attack Judith. Which looked exactly like the one you're holding, by the way."

Elisabetta's eyes widened. "That *is* strange."

The silence stretched out between us.

"Where did you get that book?" I asked.

"It was a gift," she said. "Calista gave it to me."

CHAPTER 16

The next day, I strolled towards my office, allowing myself to ponder once again the questions I'd been wrestling with all night long. Why did the symbol seem to point to my cousin? And why did anyone I asked about the symbol tell me they didn't know what it meant? There were too many of them to be merely coincidental. Then again, just because a symbol kept showing up didn't necessarily mean it was dangerous — did it?

I wandered over to the large elm between Crandall and Randsworth Halls to see if I could find the statue Nate had mentioned when we'd visited the fountain. I stepped into the shade of the massive tree — its thick trunk exploded above into an eerie tangle of stark, empty branches — and circled around until I found a statue of a woman in a veil, about four feet high and carved from white stone. She wasn't holding a bird in her raised right hand, as Nate had said, but a feather, and it was poised over a small square bottle next to her feet. Her left hand, which was by her side, held a rectangular shape like a tablet or an open book. It appeared the mysterious woman had been writing with a quill, but had paused or had been interrupted or was waiting for something. Her blank stone eyes were haunting.

I moved back onto the sidewalk and walked quickly to Crandall, shivering, grateful for the sun on my shoulders again.

Several of my students leaving the building said hello as I stepped to the side to allow them to exit. Seeing them reminded me that I needed to catch up on my grading and prepare the following week's lecture. There was plenty to do to keep my mind off of recent events. I resolved not to think about the symbol for a few hours, if I could help it.

As I climbed up to the English department floor, I passed Norton talking animatedly with Spencer. They stopped speaking when I went by, though they both nodded a greeting. The awkward silence seemed to fill up the hallway, prompting me to scurry to my office.

I angled the key at the door lock, then

noticed it was already open, just barely. That was odd — I always locked it. Maybe one of the cleaning crew forgot to pull it shut all the way. After I pushed it open, I couldn't process what I was seeing at first.

The desk and bookshelves had been knocked over and the file cabinet was on its side. Books and papers were scattered everywhere, and the top of my desk was smeared with crimson, in the shape of a crude rose. A network of red thorny branches with jagged edges covered most of the far office wall. Was that paint? Or blood?

I screamed, grabbing at the doorframe as my knees buckled.

Spencer and Norton ran down the hallway, stopping short at the sight of the mess inside the room. Spencer gently pulled me out of the office and propped me up against the hallway bulletin board. I could feel the edge of a poster cutting into my neck but didn't seem to have the energy to move away. He looked deeply into my eyes.

"This is not right," he said. "Don't worry. We'll figure it out." Spencer glanced at Norton, who confirmed he was already dialing campus police on his cell phone, then back at me. "Lila, are you okay? Do you need a drink of water?"

I couldn't answer. My knees shook as I

concentrated on breathing.

He nodded and began propelling me down the hallway to the main office. "Yes, let's get you a drink, I think. Maybe something stronger than water if we have it."

Norton called from behind us, "I'll bring her bag and keys."

"Don't touch anything!" Spencer called back.

"Why? She brought them into the room after this was already done."

"No, you can't touch anything," Spencer insisted.

"But her bag isn't part of anything, so why not —"

"Because," Spencer boomed with authority. Then his shoulders slumped and he continued, sounding defeated, "You're just not supposed to touch anything."

Typically, that was about as much as English professors were expected to know about crime scenes. And I really didn't want to learn any more.

Spencer set me up in the main office, along with the promised water, although I was shaking too hard to hold it without spilling. He gently removed it from my untrustworthy fingers and set it carefully on Millicent's desk. I was vaguely worried about water stains but couldn't seem to figure out what to use as a coaster — my brain was working too slowly. Millicent took care of that herself, sliding a folded-up tissue underneath. She had an inquiring expression.

"I'm fine," I told her. She nodded and retreated to another corner of the room. It had to be bothering her that Spencer had commandeered her territory, but she didn't show her irritation, for once. Thank goodness for small favors.

Soon thereafter, I was treated to another lengthy session with Detective Archer, who all but accused me of trashing the office to steer suspicion away from myself. I could understand why he was distrustful since I kept showing up at crime scenes. But I was the victim here. Didn't that count for something?

I stressed the existence of witnesses in Spencer and Norton. I hoped they would be able to explain the sincerity of my surprise upon seeing the office for the first time.

Though what were they whispering about when I first went up the stairs? Norton had told Calista she'd pay for Roland, hadn't he? Maybe he'd decided to take it out on me instead.

Enough, I told myself. There was an explanation for all of this. I just hadn't discovered it yet. I had to stop thinking everyone was up to something nefarious — or at least stop feeling as though the environment was unusual: academia is chock full of gossip, malice, and treacherous plots. Just like any other über-competitive place.

Then again, on this campus there was a body count.

The next afternoon, I met Spencer in the main office, as requested.

He gave me a cautious smile. "Lila, how are you?"

"Feeling better."

"Good, good. Glad to hear it. We took care of your office — painted the wall, put in a new desk and everything has been, er, cleaned up," he said. He removed a small envelope from his pocket, which he held out to me. "We also had the lock redone — here's your new key."

Relief swept through me. I hadn't even thought about having to deal with the office and here it was already done. I thanked him, and he waved his hand to indicate that it was nothing. "I'm so very sorry you had to endure such a thing. If there is anything I can do to help you move forward from this, please let me know."

I expressed my gratitude again as he, in the dignified way he always had about him, took his leave. Then I headed down the hall, fighting the flicker of anxiety welling up the closer I got to my door.

Inside, the office was pristine, aside from the piles of papers on my desk that some kind soul had picked up and stacked neatly for me. I'd have to re-file them, but at least the red wall marks were gone. It was almost impossible to imagine that anything horrifying had ever happened here. I opened the window to let in some fresh air to counter the strong new-paint smell. I was impressed that facilities had been willing to repaint the wall overnight. Spencer must have some pull over there.

Before tackling the filing project, I booted up the laptop and turned on some Bach, whom I usually find calming. It would be good to at least aim for tranquil before any advisees arrived, and I did not want to let yesterday's ominous warning control me — even though I was scared, I wasn't going to act like it.

In fact, maybe I should hang the rose-and-thorn necklace on my office door as a sort of reverse psychology declaration. That would show whoever was responsible that their effort to scare me had failed.

Or it might get me killed.

After completing the filing, advising several students, and plowing through one grading stack, I was exhausted.

My cell rang, and I was surprised to find Detective Archer on the other end. He said he was in the neighborhood — why do people feel compelled to say that when they want to stop by? — and had a follow-up question about the incident today. I agreed to his visit. Three minutes later, he knocked on my office door.

I guess he really was in the neighborhood.

I invited him in, indicating the student chair next to my desk. He set down a brown canvas field bag overflowing with papers. I deduced from the way the pages were bent at the corners that someone had been doing a lot of examination.

He flipped open his black notepad and reviewed a few pages, running his free hand across his short black hair. I waited patiently. Finally, he gave me a smile that was far more neutral than friendly. Professional, if I had to call it something. Meant to put me at ease.

I wasn't at ease.

"Yesterday you said you couldn't think of

anyone who might have had a grudge against you."

"Yes."

"Let's dig into that a little bit more," he said.

"Okay." I reflected. Still came up empty. "I haven't been here very long, so I have no idea what I could have done to upset some-one."

"How about Tad Ruthersford?"

I was stunned. "Not that I know of. He's been very welcoming to me."

"Ever hear him talk negatively about anyone else in the department?"

"Just, you know, normal gossip. Nothing out of the ordinary."

When it became clear I wasn't going to offer any examples, he nodded. "Let's try something else. Tell me more about your relationship with your cousin."

"We grew up together."

"Did she ever confide in you?"

"Sure. All the time."

I stopped short — maybe emphasizing how close we were wasn't a good idea. He'd already insinuated that I'd performed the office vandalism myself. It was only a short leap to a worse accusation, like being an ac-complice to Roland's murder, which he probably thought already. My palms were sweaty. I didn't know why he always made me feel guilty when I knew I wasn't, but he was good at it.

"Did she ever say anything about Roland?"

"She did," I said warily.

He waited.

"She thought he was mean."

He wrote that down.

"What made her think he was mean?"

"He was very critical. Rude. Unkind." I gestured vaguely. "Et cetera."

"Would you agree with that assessment?"

I sighed. "Yes. But she was just venting. Everyone complained about his behavior. What does this have to do with my office?"

"We're looking for connections."

I could see his reasoning. "But why are you focusing on Calista? She couldn't have done anything to my office because she's in jail."

"Who says she has to be working alone?"

That was a scary thought, but I shook my head firmly. "If there was someone working with her, they wouldn't go after me. She wouldn't let them."

"Them?"

"Whoever. You're the one who proposed the group scenario, not me."

He tapped his pen on the desk top.

"What about the symbol on the book you showed me? Those elements were in my office too . . . there was a rose on my desk and the thorns painted on the wall." I decided not to tell him about the other places I'd found it, for now anyway. He seemed more interested in gathering evidence against my cousin than in helping her, and until I understood what the symbol meant, I'd keep a few things to myself.

"You forgot the tattoo."

"What tattoo?"

"On your cousin's back."

"What in the world are you talking about?"

The detective pulled a manila envelope out of his field bag and shuffled through some photographs. He placed one on the table between us. It was a clear shot: an expanse of skin with a dark red and black tattoo about four inches long that matched the emblem I kept seeing everywhere. "This is a picture of Calista's back."

"I've never seen that tattoo."

"It's recent," he said. "According to your cousin."

"She told you that?"

"It was noted when she was processed, but yes, she confirmed it was new."

"Maybe she just picked it off the menu at

the tattoo shop." It sounded weak even as I said it, but I desperately wanted to believe it. "Have you checked out wherever she had it done?"

"Yes, but they said she brought it in. And we found the design for it on her laptop."

He watched my reaction. I'm sure it said that Calista and I were going to have a long talk.

CHAPTER 17

I sat in my office, staring at the wall. The vandalism incident, along with the detective's revelations, had shaken me, and I was having trouble concentrating on the reading in front of me.

Why did Calista have a tattoo of the rose-and-thorn symbol? And why was it showing up at crime scenes? And why did no one admit to knowing what it meant? I couldn't fit the information into any coherent explanation. As if that wasn't enough, Detective Archer had actually said that I should let him know if I planned to leave town — *that* I recognized from countless movies as the line no one is happy to hear. My mind was racing.

"So what are you wearing to the Halloween party?" I turned to see Nate standing in the doorway. He was holding a literature anthology easily in one hand, which was remarkable, given that they ran to well over a thousand pages each. They inflamed my carpal tunnel even when I used two hands.

"I'm not going," I said. Although I had received the engraved invitation sent by the chancellor to all faculty members, I planned to spend the evening handing out candy to children. It was not my favorite holiday by any means, and I thought it would be wise to stay out of the chancellor's line of vision as much as possible this semester.

Nate walked into my office and settled himself on the chair next to my desk. "Oh no, Professor. You have to go. It's the social event of the year."

"Not after what happened to my office."

"That was brutal. I get it. But I'll go with you to the party. No one is going to mess with these guns." Nate pointed to one of his biceps. "Don't let the small size fool you."

I laughed. "That's a kind offer, but I don't have anything to wear anyway."

"That doesn't matter, Lila, because it's not so much a party as a command performance. Everyone goes. And I swear the chancellor has someone taking attendance."

"Really?"

"Well, one year Tad didn't go and it was mentioned more than once, if you know what I mean. And you remember what happened to him with Roland and tenure and whatnot. Not that they are necessarily connected . . . but they could be."

"Speaking of Tad, the detective asked me about him."

Nate nodded. "They've been questioning him."

"That's weird."

"I thought you said the detective talked to you again too."

"Yes, but I went to him with some additional information."

He considered this. "Well, I hope they're just trying to be thorough."

"You don't think Tad —"

"No way."

He looked down at the anthology and aimlessly flipped a few of the pages. "Anyway, back to the party. You must find something to wear."

"What are you wearing?" I tried to turn the question around.

"Well, it's literary." He grinned. "And that's all I'm saying."

The theme of the event was Great Characters in Literature, which hardly seemed fair to all the other departments in the university but the chancellor had been an English professor once upon a time. At least it was something I could work with on short notice

— unlike, say, Great Elements of the Periodic Table.

I sighed. "I'll look for something."

Nate seemed relieved. "Good. We will amuse ourselves with running commentary about other people's costume choices."

I agreed to meet him at the fountain before proceeding to the party, which would be held in Randsworth Hall on Saturday. He gave me a friendly salute and left.

I surveyed the novel titles on my shelves to see if they'd prompt any costume concepts, but no immediate solutions sprang to mind. Everything was still wildly out of order but at least the books were no longer strewn across the floor, thanks to whoever had painted the office. I'd have to go home and peruse my existing wardrobe for ideas.

I stopped in the main office on my way out to grab my mail. In the middle of the stack was another typed letter instructing me to wear the engraved necklace to the upcoming Halloween party and warning me again to tell no one.

A chill penetrated my body, but it was pierced with heat. The combination of anxiety and anger was overwhelming. I crumpled the letter, shoved it deep into my bag, and ran down the stairs into the sunlight.

On the front porch of Crandall, I stood still, taking deep breaths to counter the tightness in my chest as I tried to think through things logically.

Someone wanted me to be seen with a symbol associated with crime scenes. Were they trying to set me up?

Or were they trying to pound the final proverbial nail into Calista's coffin?

Wrong image.

Totally wrong image.

I shook my head to clear it.

My eyes scanned the campus, where students and faculty members meandered to their usual destinations. None of them appeared remotely frightened. I wanted that to be me.

Who was sending these messages? It had to be someone who was going to the Halloween party. Though Nate had said everyone did, so that didn't help. The anonymity only made the notes more disturbing.

Would it make things better or worse for Calista if I went to the police with the letters and the necklace? I was paralyzed by indecision.

As I walked along the campus sidewalk on Friday, I was comforted by the sight of individuals scattered around the steps of various university buildings, speaking animatedly. It was as if they had been staged to represent the best kind of scene in academe. Presumably they were talking about intelligent things — and enthusiastic about them too. More likely, they were discussing the social events of the weekend, but one couldn't tell that from afar. I felt a small and surprising glow of pleasure about having landed this job, recent terrors aside. I'd decided to ignore the anonymous note for now.

Pennington Library loomed regally over the sidewalk. It was an imposing and beautiful building, almost a block long, built of granite slabs and fronted by massive carved columns. Even this late in the fall, there were two clusters of tall deep red and purple flowers, with a lower row of yellow ones in front, on either side of the entrance. I didn't know the names of any of the plants; I had never been a gardener — more from a lack of time than interest.

Things had been so busy since the semester began that I hadn't had a chance to check out the library, and I was eager to see what Pennington had to offer. I ascended the steep stairway and passed the metal electrical gates designed to prevent book theft, heading over to study the large map displayed next to the checkout desk.

Someone called my name. I turned to see Willa bearing down on me like a ship cutting through waves. She coasted to a stop.

"Hi, Willa." I smiled at her. "Do you teach a class in the library?"

"Just here for an assessment meeting. Norton could only get Addison to volunteer, turns out. I agreed to serve after all. I'd thought he could manage something as simple as rounding up two other people for this project, but apparently not." She tilted her head, causing the pile of chestnut curls heaped on top to slide dangerously near the side. They stopped short of actually plunging off. "Not many people enjoy Norton's management style."

I thought back to his behavior at the memorial service and understood completely.

"Have you seen them? We were supposed to convene in one of the upstairs rooms, but neither has showed up yet."

"Sorry." I shook my head. "What time's the meeting?"

"Now." She checked her watch. "Oh, I am a wee bit early, I suppose. Best return and try to be patient. Are you here for Isabella Dare work today?"

I shook my head. "Just trying to learn my

way around the library." At the sight of disappointment on her face, I added, "For future research."

"Well," she said, smoothing back an errant curl, "it's essential."

"For tenure. I know."

It was important to show that I knew what was expected of me.

"I meant for literary history. You have such an opportunity to make a difference, to educate the rest of the world about the words of Ms. Dare."

Now I felt stupid about the tenure comment.

"Let me ask you, Lila," she said, dropping her voice. "Do you have a press in mind for publishing her work? And, of course, your scholarship on her work?"

"No," I said, knowing I should be saying yes.

"I may have some ideas for you. Once you have a proposal ready, let's meet for tea. My treat. Just ring me when you're ready."

"How kind — thank you. I will absolutely take you up on that."

We exchanged phone numbers and Willa sailed away, the hem of her violet tunic fluttering behind in her wake.

I marched upstairs, newly determined, and found some critical studies that might provide useful context for my proposal. In a vacant carrel, I plopped them onto the desk and sighed deeply. Almost instantly, the mere sight of all of those pages wearied me. It seemed too soon to go wholly back into scholarship mode, that single-purposed realm of exhaustive activity. It had only been a few months since I'd finished the dissertation itself, and I'd needed time to decompress from that stress. But one must do what is required, as Judith would say, when one is probationary faculty. I picked up a book and began reading. Within an hour, I'd recognized that the books wouldn't be as helpful as I'd thought, and I deposited them on the reshelving cart.

On my way downstairs, I remembered the folder I'd found in the main office. Since I was here, perhaps I should dig into Poe Collins. At the bottom, I veered over to the row of computers housing the library's catalog. There was only one free. As I reached for the keyboard, the man next to me looked over, and I realized it was Eldon. I greeted him, and he stared blankly at me. I pushed away the powerful wave of déjà vu — both Higginses had perfected the ability to project utter indifference and alpha position in one glance — and introduced myself. Once he was in possession of name, rank, and department information, he rewarded me with a curt nod.

"I haven't had a chance to tell you that I'm sorry about your loss," I said. Although I hadn't particularly liked Roland, I hadn't wished him ill either.

"Thank you," he said gruffly. He pushed his glasses higher on his nose. They were so smudged I wondered how he could see through them.

"Doing some research?"

"Evidently," he said, turning back to his computer and hitting a few keys. Yep, there was the Higgins family charm in action.

"What are you working on?"

He sighed and kept pecking at his keyboard. "This and that."

I received the Go Away message loud and clear, but I wanted to know more about Eldon. The display at the department meeting had suggested he was very much like Roland. But was that how he normally operated? What made him tick?

I tried again. "Article or book?"

"Just tying up loose ends on something my brother and I were working on," he said vaguely, bending closer to squint at something on the screen.

"Oh, did you collaborate often?"

"Sometimes," he said, making a note on

the legal pad next to him with a Waterford pen.

"You're a Renaissance scholar too, right?"

He turned to me, his eyes glowing. "Oh, have you read my work?"

Awkward.

"Not yet," I said. "Though I look forward to it."

A small chime indicated that his window was about to time out, and he went back to the computer, wiggled the mouse, and began typing more purposefully.

"I should get to work too," I said. "Have fun."

He sniffed in response.

I quickly pulled up the library database search page and typed Poe Collins's name into the box, which yielded five articles in scholarly journals. None of the articles were accessible in full text for downloading, but two of them were available in physical form in the library stacks. I'd have to make copies of those and send away for the rest through interlibrary loan if I wanted to read them.

I took a picture of the necessary call numbers with my cell and consulted the library map again. The stacks were located two floors down. I crossed the main floor, past the circulation desk, which was humming with activity, and took the elevator. When the doors slid open with a cheery ding, I stepped out into the room, which was packed with shelves as far as the eye could see. Taking a moment to figure out the flow of numbers on the end markers, I moved in the direction of the area housing literary journals. It was eerily quiet and empty compared to the floor I'd just left, which was bustling with students and library staff. Most stacks felt like cemeteries anyway, and in a sense they were — filled to the brim with materials used by fewer and fewer people in this digital age. I walked a little faster to counter the spookiness. After a few minutes, I located the appropriate row at the far side of the building and slowed to browse the titles, my hand trailing along the metal shelf until I found the exact volume and issue I needed. I tucked the journal under my arm and checked my phone for the other call number.

A door creaked slowly, then closed abruptly with a metallic clank that echoed throughout the room. My muscles tensed. Although I knew it was most likely another scholar in search of an archived text, I was wary these days. I stood still, listening hard. There were no footsteps. Someone must have been leaving, not arriving. My shoulders relaxed and I returned to my slow crawl along the row, checking the tags on each shelf for the number I needed.

As I pulled the second journal from the shelf, a rumble followed by a crash filled the room. Then another. Then a third. I ran down the long rows as fast as I could, panic rising in my chest, and jabbed the elevator button repeatedly. A quick glimpse over my shoulder revealed that the shelves at the end were falling against each other like dominos, having been pushed exactly towards where I had been standing.

CHAPTER 18

Upstairs, I darted over to the circulation desk staff and told them what had happened. Campus security was summoned to check things out. After filling out a report that basically said I saw shelves falling, I was excused from the conversation. I quickly made photocopies of the articles at the library machines and dropped the journals off at the front desk. There was no way I was going back to the stacks tonight.

As I was walking home, my cell rang. The recorded voice told me to press one if I was willing to accept a call from an inmate at Stonedale Department of Corrections. I did so and was connected with Calista's voice.

We talked for a few minutes, and I filled her in on the office and library incidents. As I related the events, a current of resentment coursed through me, though I didn't know where to aim it or who was behind either of them. All I could think was *enough already.*

I was so wrapped up in the heat of the emotion that I only caught the tail end of what Calista was saying.

". . . I'm so worried about you."

"Likewise. Hey, why didn't you tell me about your tattoo?"

She didn't say anything.

"Detective Archer found it significant," I prodded. I could hear muted noises in the background. Sounded like an escalating argument. I wondered how dangerous it was for her in there.

She coughed for extended period of time. "Maybe we could talk about this in person, Lil."

I had heard that prison phone calls were taped. Maybe that weird cough was code for shut up. But I was angry that she wouldn't disclose what was going on.

"You said you couldn't tell me what the symbol meant, so it must mean something."

"It's just ink. I saw the design on the knife and thought it was cool." Her exasperation was clear, but now that she was giving up some details, I wasn't going to stop pushing.

"So you got a tattoo?"

"I was experimenting with branding."

"Branding? Like on a ranch?"

She laughed. "No. Branding as in building

my authorial product. I was even going to put the symbol on my next book cover."

"But I've seen it in other places too. And what about the necklace? Why didn't you tell me this when I showed you —"

"I made some necklaces, yes. It's no big deal."

"It actually is a big deal. The detective is building a case against you because of the symbols. Why would he do that unless they meant something else? Can you tell me?"

"I just did. And you're seriously stressing me out, Lil. Could we drop it, please?"

I dropped it.

After a minute, I asked how things were going.

She said things were atrocious.

Then the timer sounded and we were disconnected.

I didn't feel very good about that conversation. And her explanation didn't explain much. If the symbol was her own new brand, why would it be embossed in books by other authors? Where did she obtain that knife? And was the necklace I'd been given one that she had made? Everything I learned only seemed to lead to more questions.

Calista's evasiveness made no sense. We both knew I could do a much better job of getting her out of jail if she would be straight with me. But I was stuck for the time being, no thanks to my cousin, and I needed to regroup.

Early Saturday morning, I was much calmer, so I read through the copies I'd made at the library. The bio at the end of both articles simply said "Poe Collins is a pseudonym for a professor at an American university." So not helpful. The articles were both attacks on newer mystery writers: the first one took culinary cozy author Dee Parkinstaff to task for "plots in dire need of resuscitation," and the second one attacked suspense writer Fain DeToro's "fatally shallow swipes at characterization." The articles demonstrated strong familiarity with the mystery genre throughout, making long-winded expeditions deep into works by other authors — from early to late, well-known and lesser-known — with a reckless disregard for showing the necessity of such forays. The footnotes, in fact, were quite a bit longer than the article itself in both cases. It was as if the author simply threw in a footnote whenever he or she thought of something, rather than using them to illustrate or reference a relevant point. The writing style alone would have garnered a "rewrite" in one of my classes.

I set them down on the sofa and opened my laptop. An internet search for Poe Collins yielded only the titles I'd already found. There weren't any articles by others referencing Collins either, though the ones I'd read were fairly recently published, and perhaps no one had written a refuting piece yet. It was only a matter of time though. Scholarship delights in rebuttals.

Cady strolled up, no doubt looking for her breakfast. After filling her food and water bowls, I settled back down on the sofa, thinking hard. Why would the folder I'd found originally be in the main office? Roland had made it clear he didn't think mysteries were worth considering as literature. Was it a pseudonym of someone on the faculty? Had Roland figured out who they were and planned to "out" them? Or perhaps he was blackmailing them. Wasn't that a strong motive for murder?

It was all very mysterious, this folder tantalizingly named "Mysteries."

I should probably tell Detective Archer about it, but how could I explain finding it? I'd never pried into something that wasn't mine like that before, and I was completely uncomfortable. So I either had to confess that I'd snooped or I'd have to lie. At this point, I didn't find either alternative appealing.

Eventually, it was time to tackle the Halloween party costume problem. I stood in my closet, reviewing available choices, which could be divided into three general categories: things that were black, things that used to be black but had faded, and a few colorful items I didn't remember buying. I pawed through the options, unearthing at last a dark yellow floor-length dress with long sleeves and a faint but distinct vertical line pattern — must have been an impulse buy, though I couldn't fathom why at this point. It would have to do. I decided not to wear the necklace. I didn't want to play along with the unknown note-writer's plan. Calista had told me not to wear it, and I trusted her.

After a quick shower and hurried walk to campus, I arrived at the fountain to discover Nate in a flowing white shirt and black trousers with a long coat and top hat. We regarded each other carefully.

"Who are you?" I asked finally. "I give up."

"Miles Coverdale from *Blithedale Romance.* Though I could be anyone, granted. It's not like he has a particularly memorable wardrobe." He angled his head, appraising my dress. "And you are . . . a sun goddess?"

I shook my head.

"A child of the corn?"

I laughed. "No. I'm the woman behind the wallpaper."

"In the Charlotte Perkins Gilman story?" Nate nodded approvingly. "Nice."

The water trickled into the fountain merrily beside us, but a sense of foreboding filled me from head to toe. "Do we have to go, Nate?"

"We do. Are you ready?" Nate pointed at Randsworth Hall, which was blazing with white and orange lights. People in fantastical costumes bustled around in front, greeting one another loudly. There were a number of performers on the grass outside of the building: skeletons juggling fiery batons, veiled ladies pantomiming distress, grim reapers wielding scythes, fairies dancing with streamers floating behind them, and so forth. Nate put his hand on the small of my back and maneuvered us through the crowd of people gawking at the spectacles.

At the top of the stone stairs, we each accepted a flute of champagne from a tuxedo-clad waiter. Nate winked at me as we both took sips.

"Friends." Tad materialized in front of us in a linen shirt and tattered brown pants, performing a melodramatic bow. "Robinson

Crusoe at your service. I figured it was metaphorically appropriate given the exile of my previous year."

Nate gave him a hearty clap on the back. "Well done, man."

We identified our own costumes, then Tad came in closer, whispering, "Wait until you see Eldon."

"Do tell," said Nate, clearly intrigued.

Tad smiled. "Ah, you'll see soon enough."

A surge of entering partygoers pushed forward, and we were caught up with them, sweeping into the high-ceilinged main hall where guests holding glasses mingled and conversed. At the far edge of the crowd, Norton was in a medieval tunic, Spencer in leather jerkin and hose, and Judith in an old-fashioned frock which I presumed had some connection to a Woolfian protagonist — Clarissa Dalloway, perhaps. We all seemed to have chosen something relevant to our areas, as was perhaps to be expected.

The walls were unoriginally swathed in orange and black, but the fabric appeared expensive, and the hundreds of crystals suspended on invisible wires from the ceiling added an elegant touch. Another waiter traded our empty champagne flutes for full ones; yet another presented a platter of tiny hors d'oeuvres, which we sampled and

251

praised. It was all very posh and delightful.

"Welcome one and all." Chancellor Wellington's voice exploded through the loudspeakers. He stood on one of the steps leading to the second floor, wearing some kind of nautical garb and holding a microphone.

"Captain Ahab," Tad informed me out of the corner of his mouth. "Wrote his dissertation on *Moby Dick*."

"Patsy and I," the chancellor nodded at a blonde middle-aged mermaid in green sequins by his side, who beamed at him, "are delighted to see you here at our annual Halloween festivities. There will be a variety of traditional activities available, so do circulate. And don't forget about the best costume award, which will be announced in due time. Enjoy, everyone."

He ended his speech with a gentlemanly flourish of the hand and passed off the microphone. As he moved to the main floor, a man in a royal costume quickly stepped up and engaged him in conversation.

Tad made a sound of disgust. "That's Eldon. Look at him sucking up to the chancellor."

"Maybe he's just wishing him a good evening," said Nate.

"Or thanking him for the job," I added.

"Doubtful." With a short laugh, Tad held

up his half-empty champagne. "But cheers to the eternal optimists."

While clinking his glass, it struck me that Tad could be right: Eldon didn't seem like the type of person who wished others a good evening or acted grateful for anything. "Who is he supposed to be?" I asked Tad.

He grinned. "You can't tell from the back, but there's a crest on the front that actually says 'Macbeth.' "

"Yeah, I don't think that was in the original play," said Nate, laughing.

A few hours later, I had chatted with colleagues galore and danced with a variety of people — including one delightful waltz with the enthusiastic Dean Okoye. I'd watched the costume judging and clapped for the winning professor of biology who had worn an elaborate steampunk-inspired suit featuring hidden panels that extended into bat wings for his transformation into Dracula.

I'd also bumped into Simone, who had informed me that she was dressed as Countess Paulina de Bassompierre from *Villette.* She glowed in a flattering gown of shimmering fabric. After I admired her attire, she snickered at mine. It wasn't as though I was very invested in my costume to begin with, but it still stung, as she intended. Conversing with Simone was like trying to dodge a tenacious bee.

Now I was hiding out with Nate by the apple-bobbing station, which was understandably ignored by party guests who had taken the time to fashion complex coiffures for their costumes. I'd never understood the appeal of plunging one's head into a cold bucket of water to grab fruit with one's teeth, anyway; it seemed both dangerous and primal, somehow.

Judith appeared, emanating cheery goodwill, as usual. "You both look divine. Are you having fun?"

We greeted her, complimented her outfit, and discussed the best costumes we'd seen.

"Well, well, well . . . what do we have here," Eldon rumbled as he joined the group. "Colleagues." He made it sound like a disease.

Everyone said hello, though it was subdued in response to his repulsive tone.

"The library staff was all abuzz after you left," he informed me.

I gave everyone a recap of the library incident.

"I've never seen a professor behave in that manner," Eldon said, radiating disapproval. "Galloping through the library like that."

I shrugged. "Adrenaline, I guess."

"First your office, now this? Things seem to be escalating," Judith said. "That's not a good sign. If it would make you feel better, you could stay with Spencer and me for as long as you like. Think about it, please, dear."

Just the thought of the unidentified menace made me cold all over.

We were quiet for a moment, then Judith changed the subject. "That is a beautiful crest on your costume, Eldon. Did you paint it yourself?"

Nate chimed in. "Interesting choice to add the label 'Macbeth' to it."

Eldon nodded. "Couldn't be bothered to explain it to this gathering of illiterati." I hardly thought university faculty could be described as illiterate, but I wasn't going to correct him. In fact, I vowed to fly under his radar henceforth if at all possible.

"I hope you have an enjoyable evening, Eldon," said Judith, choosing to overlook his discourteousness.

"Please. This is just a necessary evil. I'd rather be at home working on my book."

"Your book?" Judith curved her lips upward, though the smile didn't reach her eyes.

Eldon made a sound of exasperation.

"Yes, my *book*. The reason I was hired?" He scrutinized the circle with an expression of disbelief. "I'm writing the definitive study on Shakespeare's identity. It's going to decimate all of the existing proposals."

"Who is Shakespeare, then?" Nate cut right to it.

Eldon's face lit up with glee to the extent that, were he a comic villain, he surely would have been described as maniacal. "Well, it's not Edward de Vere, as my brother mistakenly thought. Or Francis Bacon, as others continue to insist despite all evidence to the contrary. The truth will shock the world."

"Who are you leaning towards?" Judith asked.

Eldon wagged his finger and tsked. "You know better than that, Judith. I won't be giving away my secrets. All I can say at this point is that the finest writer in the English language is not a woman." He snorted. "Of course."

Nate opened his mouth to retort but Judith subtly shook her head.

"And right on cue — it's the Three Witches," Eldon sneered. We all turned around to see Willa, Elisabetta, and Millicent talking by the far wall. Willa was clad in some sort of dark purple tunic trimmed with crystal beading over flowing pants that weren't much different from what she normally wore: she tended to exude a high priestess vibe even on a regular day. Elisabetta and Millicent both wore suits — though Elisabetta's was tailored and smart while Millicent's was another one of the shapeless, boxy brown things she favored. None of them even remotely resembled a witch.

"Really, Eldon," Judith said.

"I was trying to keep it Shakespearean, Judith. Would you prefer the three *bitches?*" Eldon gave a curt laugh. "I'm fine with that descriptor as well."

"No. I do not prefer —" Judith began.

"Look at them," Eldon interrupted her. "Working out their next spell, no doubt."

"Pardon me, Eldon, but have you ever had a conversation with any of those women?" I admired Judith's ability to keep her composure.

"I heard enough about them from my brother."

"Well, Roland did have strong opinions, but you might want to get to know them on your own."

"Hardly," Eldon said. "I have neither the desire nor the need. I respect my brother's judgment completely. And you saw how

Willa behaved in the department meeting."

"Willa was just trying to pass a course," Judith said. Her voice was still calm, but her eyes blazed.

"A less than historically significant one, yes." Eldon attempted to stare down Judith, which resulted in a draw.

"Does Millicent usually come to faculty parties? She doesn't seem very happy," I said to Judith, intentionally ignoring Eldon. That was the best thing to do with bullies, I'd heard.

"Spencer always escorts her to the Halloween party. It's a tradition that began when she came to work for Stonedale. I forget why he brought her the first time, but she always attends, even though she refuses the costume aspect. She adores him."

"That's very nice," I said. I thought back to the flowers I'd seen on Millicent's desk with the "B" card. Spencer wouldn't cheat on Judith, would he? I couldn't imagine it, but you just never know. Stranger things have happened. Since Judith didn't seem concerned about it, I chose not to worry either.

Willa and the other women headed our way.

Eldon was craning his neck so he could

watch something behind them. "Oh, here comes the dean. I must go say hello." He acted as if he were the host of the party and needed to welcome everyone personally.

"Holy crap," said Nate, once Eldon was out of earshot. "He's unbelievable!"

I watched Eldon disappear down a side hallway, the hem of his robe sweeping regally behind him. He hadn't spoken to the dean after all. Perhaps he simply enjoyed stirring the pot and fleeing. Some people were like that.

"And did you hear him say he was hired because of his book?" Nate laughed. "He's totally delusional."

Elisabetta gave us all hugs, and Judith complimented her jacket, which had an elegant bronze embroidered pattern around the hem.

"Thank you! It's one of my favorites — I decided that being retired meant I didn't have to play the costume game anymore."

Willa laughed. "I rebelled too. I fail to see the point in dressing up offstage." That explained her outfit — or lack thereof — as well.

Millicent stood slightly apart from us, as if unwilling to engage. I asked if she was having a good time. She nodded, a small — shy? — smile on her face, though she didn't say anything. I moved over to make room for her, but she remained where she was, watching the band.

Well, I tried.

"So what was Eldon talking about?" Willa asked.

"Or maybe we don't want to know," suggested Elisabetta.

The women huddled closer together for discussion purposes. Just then, I felt a tap on my shoulder. A smiling Nate requested a dance. Despite my protests, he pulled me on to the floor for a tango.

After a half hour on the dance floor, we took a break at a table near the bar and drank ice water. It was becoming increasingly stuffy in the room and, although I'd enjoyed dancing with Nate, I was exhausted and ready to go. I didn't see anyone else from the department in the immediate vicinity, so I suggested it was good time to make a break for it. Nate agreed, so we made our way through the crowd and exited. The air outside was immediately refreshing — I leaned against one of the front columns and rested my head. Nate leaned too, and we enjoyed the cool night for a few moments before the door opened and Judith emerged, her expression uncharacteristically tense.

"Oh, thank goodness. Could you two help me?" She waved us over. "Quickly, please?"

"What happened?" Nate asked, as we hurried inside.

"It's Willa," Judith said over her shoulder. "I told her what Eldon said and she was furious. She went to find him, and now I can't seem to locate her."

Nate and I quickened our pace.

"What did you tell her?" I asked, catching up with Judith.

"I shouldn't have said anything. But I thought the 'witches and bitches' exchange was odd, so I mentioned it. And instantly regretted it. I've never seen her so angry. I'm worried about what she might have planned."

I hid a smile. What was a drama professor going to do, anyway — soliloquize him into submission?

Then I reconsidered. Maybe Judith knew something about Willa that I didn't. And given the intensity of the argument between Eldon and Willa in the department meeting, perhaps some trepidation was to be expected.

"Did she say where she was going?" I heard myself ask — stupidly. Obviously if Judith knew, she wouldn't be looking for her.

"No. She just launched off. I've texted, called, and searched everywhere. Went outside to check as a last resort."

"I saw Eldon over there before." I pointed to the hallway where he had disappeared, and Judith strode purposefully forward in that direction. Pushing through the crowd, I heard Nate apologize to someone behind me. I'd already bumped into at least five people trying to keep up with Judith. Finally, we hit the dance floor, which offered spaces between gyrating couples, allowing us to move faster to the other side and over to the hallway.

Judith sped ahead. Although I was racing to keep up, she was far enough in front of me that I couldn't see her after she turned the corner — though I did hear a scream echo back through the hallway.

Nate and I sprinted around the corner to where Tad, his costume stained with dark red marks, stood perfectly still, appearing dazed. Blood slowly spread across the marble floor, away from its source: Eldon lying motionless, a wooden stake through his heart.

CHAPTER 19

The police arrived in a matter of minutes. Detective Archer strode in, shooting me a scowl that seemed to indicate an unhappy amount of suspicion. I couldn't believe Judith and I were once again early on a scene involving the Higgins brothers and stabbing. I was pretty sure he was thinking the same thing.

I knew I wasn't responsible, but what about Willa? Or Judith, for that matter, as much as I didn't want to entertain the idea? And why was Tad here with Eldon? Where had Tad been all night, anyway?

I shook my head to refocus and peered over at Nate and Tad, who were like grim bookends leaning against the wall on either side of Judith, who was fanning herself with her hand. The men were both silent and staring blankly ahead.

Suddenly, Willa burst around the corner and flew over to us, her curls waving in the air. "What's going on?"

Judith led Willa down the hallway, turning her back to us. She lowered her voice and spoke earnestly. I wondered at the need for secrecy.

"Dr. Maclean?" Detective Archer signaled for me to follow him into a nearby classroom, where I sat in the first student desk I bumped into. He settled on the teacher's desk, an enigmatic expression on his face, notepad at the ready. "So. We meet once again at a murder scene. Care to explain yourself?"

I opened my mouth but nothing came out.

"Let me rephrase that: explain yourself."

Even though I knew I was innocent, I felt confused, somehow, as if being involved so many times did in fact indicate something. "I don't know why this keeps happening. I'm starting to think maybe I'm cursed."

"I'm sure the other residents of Stonedale are wondering about you too. But let's leave that alone for the time being and talk about what you're doing here tonight."

"I came for the party, same as everyone else."

His eyes bore into mine. "Yes, but everyone else didn't find another dead body."

"Wrong place, wrong time. Again."

He rubbed the hand holding a pen over

his face and sighed. I couldn't tell if he was frustrated with me specifically or with the situation in general. "I don't know how one person can be in so many of the exactly wrong places at the exactly wrong times."

"I don't either. It's extremely upsetting."

We looked at each other until he raised one finger and made the spinning motion universally recognized as the signal to Get On With It.

"Sorry. Okay, Nate and I were leaving the party, and Judith asked us to help her." I didn't want to point the finger at Willa again, as I felt I'd done when Judith was attacked at her house. Though I couldn't be sure Willa wasn't involved either. Still, these people were the closest thing to friends I had at Stonedale, and I didn't want to be accusatory without any basis.

"Help her with what?"

"Finding someone."

He sighed again. "And this would be . . . ?"

I couldn't see a way out of it. "Willa."

His pen scribbled away. "So Judith was searching for Willa and you accompanied her into the building."

"Yes."

"And?" He sounded annoyed at having to prompt me this time.

"We walked through the hallway and

found Eldon. Then Nate called the police, who apparently called you, and here we are."

He made a note. "Dr. Maclean, you don't seem very sad about Dr. Higgins's passing."

"I am. Of course I'm upset that someone died. I'm just . . . processing."

The detective nodded briskly. "Were you close to the victim?"

Here we go again. "No."

"How did you know him?"

"He was a colleague." I knew Archer already knew that. Was he trying to trick me?

"Did you like him?" He leaned forward.

I needed to tread carefully here. "I didn't know him very well at all."

"How would you describe him?"

I wished I had nicer things to say about the Higgins brothers. "Um . . . abrasive."

"How so?"

"He seemed to enjoy saying things that upset other people."

More scribbling. I would love to see what those pages said.

"What people?"

"Pretty much everyone. He lacked tact. Like his brother."

"Can you give me an example?"

I described the department meeting show-down and the harsh comments he had made at the party. The detective waited for me to say more, but when I didn't continue, he snapped the notepad shut and slid off the desk. "That's it for now — you can go fill out the paperwork for your statement with the officer in the hallway. But I may need to talk to you again later."

Oh, how I dreaded those words.

After Nate gave his statement, we walked slowly across the green. The moon shone dully through the twisted branches of trees towering along the edges of campus. They appeared downright menacing.

"Are you okay?" I asked.

"I guess." He peered at me. "How about you?"

"Stunned. Confused. Scared."

"With good reason. I can't believe this keeps happening."

"The detective pointed that out too, especially the part about me finding the victims. I'm nervous that they think I'm involved."

Nate put his arm around me and gave me a squeeze, his soapy scent pleasantly noticeable. "I know you're not. And remember that Judith has found two as well. Tad and I have one each to our name now." He paused. "That sounds weird, but you know

267

what I mean."

"Yes, and I'm grateful." I was also surprised at how soothing his hug had been, but I'd have to explore that emotion at a future time.

"Lila, if they thought you were responsible, you'd be in jail with Calista. And given the way they just found Tad, splashed with Eldon's blood . . . well . . ." He paused for a long time. "I actually think Tad is headed to jail too."

"Do you think he did it?" I peeked sideways at him.

He shook his head vigorously. "I know he looks guilty as hell, but I'd be shocked if that were true. Tad isn't violent. At least I've never observed any sign of that."

"I guess we'll have to see. Can I ask you something else?"

"Of course."

"How well do you know Willa?"

"Just since I came here last year."

"Has she ever given you a reason to worry about anything?"

He sounded puzzled. "Worry? In what way?"

"I don't know. I just . . ." I realized I either had to tell him everything or stop talking, because it wouldn't make any sense in bits and pieces. I was tired of trying to sort this out on my own. It was time I confided in someone, and Nate it would be. Damn the consequences.

I stopped walking and gripped his arm so he would pause as well. "There's something going on at Stonedale. Something strange. I can't quite figure out how it all fits together. But obviously someone is attacking people. And I keep seeing these weird symbols everywhere. Did you notice that the stake tonight had a symbol carved on it?"

"I did see something. I asked the detective about it, in fact, but he wouldn't say anything."

"The same design was also on the knife used to kill Roland and on the book used to attack Judith."

"All three?" Nate's jaw dropped.

"And other things too —"

"Whoa, hold on. You're going to have to spell this out for me. Start from the beginning."

I filled him in.

"What did Judith say when you asked her about it?"

"That the symbol didn't mean anything to her."

"And Elisabetta?"

"Same thing, only she claimed the book was a gift from Calista."

"And how did Calista explain the symbol?"

"Initially, she said she couldn't tell me anything at all. She was protecting someone. But then she said she saw the symbol for the first time on that knife and liked it, so she was going to use it as a signature image for her authorial brand." It still didn't make sense to me. First it was supposedly a big secret and later it was only about marketing? Didn't add up.

"You don't think Calista —"

"No," I said. "But I can't explain why everything keeps leading back to her either."

We started walking again by tacit agreement and continued the rest of the way in silence, both lost in thought. When we arrived at my house, I invited him to come in for coffee, but he declined, for which I was grateful. I was almost too tired to stand upright. We made plans to meet the next morning for breakfast. I stumbled through my evening routine, collapsed onto the bed, and was out immediately.

A few hours later, a cold gust of wind struck my face, and I gasped, pitching myself upright. The curtains were billowing, rain was pouring in, and Cady was yowling on the windowsill.

Confused, I stumbled from the bed to close the window. A flash of movement caught my eyes and I pressed my face against the screen. I could just barely make out a figure running across my lawn, away from my house. Terrified but also furious, I called out to whoever it was. Like they were going to return and explain. I gently moved Cady to the floor, thanking her for being such a good watchcat. I thought briefly about calling the police but knew I couldn't deal with them again tonight.

So instead, I slammed the window shut, locked it, and went to lie on the sofa where eventually, out of sheer exhaustion, I managed to get a few hours of sleep.

In the light of day, things were less surreal: sunshine streaming through the café windows, Nate across the table, scrambled eggs and hot coffee in front of us both. Even at nine a.m. on a Sunday, Scarlett's was crowded with animated undergraduates and other residents of Stonedale. It was just the thing to counter the horror of last night. I told Nate about my nocturnal visitor, and he was upset that I hadn't called the police.

"At first I thought I dreamed it," I said. "But the carpet was still damp this morning, so the rain actually did come in."

"Someone must have opened your window from the outside." He was noticeably concerned. "You should report it."

"You're probably right, but I don't know if I can face Detective Archer again for a while."

"Lila, if he thought you were responsible, he would charge you."

"Right. But he seems to think I know what's going on for some reason." I sighed. "Wish I *did* know what's going on."

"Oh wait. Can't believe I didn't lead with this. I'm still groggy after last night." Nate set his coffee mug on the table and cleared his throat. "I have bad news. Tad's been arrested."

"What? When?"

"They charged him last night."

My thoughts flew back over the encounters I'd had with Tad so far. My gut told me he was innocent. Not that my gut had a lot of experience in identifying criminals.

"I know I asked you last night, but now that he's been charged, do you think Tad is capable of killing someone?" I hoped Nate would confirm my assessment.

"Of course not."

"I don't think so either."

"But the judge denied his bail," he said. "Which isn't a good sign."

"Already?"

"I guess so."

"I didn't know it could happen so fast. Took longer for Calista. Though she did say she'd heard the judge was a friend of Roland's. Maybe that has something to do with it. Maybe he knew Eldon too. Or maybe Tad was right when he said they suspected him all along — and they were building a case against him the whole time."

He shrugged.

"Or maybe it's just how things work here. Small town rules."

"Stonedale does seem to have its own way of operating," I said. "When can we go see him?"

"Not until we're approved. Tad has to put us on a list, and they have to do a background check, blah blah blah. I've spoken to his father, who may be able to pull some strings and rush it. I'll keep you posted. But for now, let's just hope he's safe in there."

I nodded. We ate for a while in silence.

"This morning I searched the internet for the symbol you described, but I couldn't find anything unusual," Nate offered, taking a bite of his eggs.

"I did that too. Thanks for trying."

Nate chewed, swallowed, and put down his fork. "Speaking of mysterious things, what was the wooden stake supposed to mean? That Eldon was a vampire?"

I thought about this. It was true that Eldon's incredibly pale skin suggested he could be one of the mythical undead who shunned sunlight, but unfortunately the same could be said for many scholars. When you spent a majority of your time researching in a dark library or writing alone in your office, that tended to happen.

"I don't know," I admitted. "But I've got to find out what the symbol inscribed on it stands for."

"Seems to me you're going to have to ask Calista about it again sooner rather than later, Lila."

"Why?"

"Because she's put the symbol on her body. Permanently."

My head ached. I stabbed at a tomato slice on my plate.

"She's your cousin — can't you ask?"

"I *have* been asking."

He drank some of the orange juice that had just arrived, delivered with apologies by a chirpy server who was endearingly frazzled by the number of customers for which she was responsible. I sipped my coffee, listening to the hum and bustle of the crowd and feeling somewhat safe for the moment.

"You know, I keep looking for answers and trying to make sense of things, but it only gets more and more confusing. I'm desperate to get Calista out of jail, but I'm running out of ideas. Maybe if we hang tight, the police will figure it out and it will all be over soon." I gave Nate a hopeful smile.

He shook his head. "No way. The killer has been successful twice. I think it's all just beginning."

CHAPTER 20

The week before Homecoming was chaotic with preparations for the book sale. The Lit Club students had been emailing and popping by my office with last-minute questions and, in some cases, subtle requests for reassurance.

Somewhere amidst the din, I called Detective Archer and left a voicemail asking if Calista would be released now that Tad had been taken into custody.

A short while later, I received a text that simply said "No."

It was worth a try. I wouldn't stop trying either.

On Wednesday afternoon, I borrowed the blue-tagged storage room key from the main office again so the students and I could bring up the books for Homecoming. The plan was to store them in Alex's van until the sale. I asked Millicent if I could hold onto the key for the next week so we could return unsold books to storage afterwards. She was surprisingly cool about it — in fact, ever since the vandalism incident, she had seemed less annoyed by my general existence, which made everything a bit easier.

Although I was not a fan of the basement, it was far less unsettling to walk down the dimly lit hallway with four chattering students beside me. They were talking about the upcoming weekend's events with excitement, and none of them seemed bothered by the gloomy basement setting. I led them over to Storage Room 12, where we spent the better part of the afternoon together, boxing and lugging books up to Alex's van.

As we loaded the last carton into the vehicle, Liane asked me about the cash box. Simone hadn't retrieved it for them yet. Surprise, surprise. Since I had the key, I told Liane I'd get the box and bring it to them on Friday night.

We said goodbye, and I headed back down to the storage room. It took some digging, but finally I found the metal box inside of a plastic container that also held a bunch of old ledger books. As I reviewed a few crumbling pages of the ledgers to make sure they weren't anything the Lit Club needed, I gradually became aware of the sound of voices, plural. With the strange acoustics of the underground, I couldn't tell where they were coming from at first, but I narrowed it down to the left. I put the books back into the container and moved over to the side of the room, sliding into a gap between two shelves and pressing my ear to the wall, straining to make out words. I couldn't tell if the speakers were male or female.

Stepping back, I noticed a metal vent about a foot up from the floor. I squatted to look through it, but the vent was aimed down on the other side, preventing me from seeing anything except cement. I tried to turn the rusty knob that controlled the angle, but it was stuck. I put my ear to the vent. The voices had taken on a unified rhythm. It sounded like chanting, as if — I realized with a chill — the people involved were in the middle of a cult ritual.

I picked up the lockbox and my bag, turned off the light, and poked my head around the doorway. No one was in the corridor. Pulling the door shut behind me, I crept along the wall until I came to the next room. That door was open a crack and light spilled out into the dim gray of the hallway. The voices were louder but not any clearer. I edged closer, trying to peer inside, but I couldn't see around the door. As I reached out to push on the wood, it slammed shut. I staggered backwards and thought for a second. My mind could only come up with two choices: 1) pound on the door and demand entrance into the scary cult room, or 2) run far, far away. I chose the latter.

On Friday evening, I set out for the brightly lit Stonedale football stadium to attend Homecoming. Cars packed the parking lots as well as the nearby streets. I wasn't a huge sports fan, but I needed to check on the Literature Club booth — I hoped it was working out well for the students. An hour or two of immersion into a joyful campus celebration seemed like a good way to recharge from the relentless stress that had invaded my life.

I shivered in my North Face coat as I walked through the wrought-iron gates with the lockbox tucked under my arm. Despite the forecast, I hadn't believed it could snow this early in the fall and had said so to my American Lit class on Wednesday. The students had assured me it could indeed happen in Colorado, where seasonal weather divisions were more a theory than a practice, and it was looking as though they were right. I hoped any snow would hold off at least until tomorrow so tonight's sale would be a success.

The student organization booths were set up along the sidewalk around the stadium. All of the tables were covered with colorful banners announcing club names, and the students working the booths were animated and engaged in conversations with potential members. I passed a number of colleagues, including Addison, Norton, and Simone — who was nowhere near the Lit Club work, it should be noted. I greeted them and called Simone over.

To protest my having summoned her, Simone was slow to respond. But I waited. I wanted her to be the one who brought the box to the students. She hadn't done a single thing to contribute to our work yet.

"Lila," she said in a baffled tone, as if she couldn't fathom what I could possibly have to say to her.

I held out the metal box. "This is for the students," I said.

"Me?" She fluttered her eyelids. "I thought you were handling it."

Like I'd handled everything so far. I swallowed the retort and summoned my most cordial tone. "It would be helpful if you would take this over to them."

She received the box in her leather-gloved hands. "Is there a key?"

"Yes," I said, "hold on." I rummaged in

my bag and felt around for the key ring. When I pulled it out, the rose-and-thorn necklace was entangled with it. I tried to quickly disengage the chain before she saw it, but it slipped out of my grasp and fell onto the ground, emblem up.

Simone gasped.

"What?" I asked, bending down to retrieve it.

She snatched the necklace from me, looking closely at the design on the disk.

"Wait —" I began.

She stared at me. "They chose *you*?"

"Who?" I asked.

"The Briar Rose Society," she whispered.

I shook my head while sorting through my confusion. A bell was going off somewhere deep in the back of my mind. Briar Rose — wasn't that the name of a folktale? "Little Briar Rose," that was it. Most people knew the version called "Sleeping Beauty." That explained why the symbol was so similar to the illustrations I'd seen online. And probably explained why it seemed familiar the first time I saw it. However, I still didn't know what the symbol was doing on a knife, book, or necklace. Not to mention why it kept showing up at crime scenes.

"I can't believe it," she went on.

"Simone, what are you talking about?"

"It's okay," she said, going into conspiratorial mode. "I know it's a secret. But you don't have to pretend with me — I know all about the society. You've been invited to join them, haven't you?"

"Mmm," I said. Simone was the first person who'd shown any indication of knowing what the symbol meant, and I was afraid if I said the wrong thing she would stop talking.

She shook the necklace slightly. "When did you get this?"

"A little while ago," I said. "Were you expecting one too?"

Simone stepped closer and spoke quietly. "My mother was a member," she confided. "I was sure I'd be selected this year."

I nodded, trying to give the impression I knew what she was talking about.

"I didn't think they contacted potential members until after they'd been here for at least a full semester," she mused, turning over the necklace. "Maybe they've changed things."

I shrugged. "I don't know much yet." Which was true, actually.

She straightened up and smiled brightly at me. "Perhaps you could put in a good word for me when the next discussion of membership comes up."

I smiled back just as brightly. "Of course." It was shocking how quickly she changed demeanors. You could almost see the wheels turning. Now that I had something she wanted — at least she thought I did — her air of condescension was melting away.

"Thank you so much, Lila," Simone said.

As I tried to think of questions to ask Simone that would simultaneously provoke the sharing of additional information but make it seem as though I actually knew something about the society, I heard my name called. I handed Simone the key and gestured for her to follow me. Fiona was waving at us from a booth farther down. She was cheerful in a red hat and wool coat combination. The table was draped with a dark cloth onto which letters spelling out the club name had been sewn in a variety of bright fabrics.

"What a wonderful drape," I said. The black provided a perfect contrast to the piles of colorful t-shirts stacked tidily along the top of the table.

"Liane made it," she said. "She's seriously gifted."

"Where is she?" I asked, checking the individuals browsing through the boxes of books lined up neatly on the ground behind the booth.

"Oh, she went to get us some cocoa. It's freezing out here." Fiona's cheeks were rosy. She rubbed her hands up and down the sleeves of her coat, trying to warm up.

"How is everything going?"

"We've sold half of our stock already," Fiona said. "Books *and* shirts."

"Well done. Do you need anything? Want me to cover for you so you can take a break?"

"I don't think so." She shook back her bangs. "It's super fun to be out here selling."

Fiona thanked me and turned to speak to a student standing next to me. I moved to the right and said hello to Alex. He looked up from the table, where he was making change for a customer, and gave me a friendly smile.

"Everything okay?"

He produced a jaunty thumbs up.

"Dr. Raleigh has the lockbox for you," I said, nodding at Simone.

She walked over and handed it to him. He began pulling bills and change from his pockets and loading the compartments within.

"Need anything?" I asked, though the words were drowned out by the din of the marching band passing by. He shook his head, so I headed to the stadium.

The sound of drums echoed in the wake of the band ahead of me, which was doing its best to motivate the crowd. I waved at Judith and Willa, who were standing by another booth. Normally I would have gone over to speak with them, but it was too loud to hold any meaningful conversation. I continued to follow the band, impressed by the number of faculty members who had shown up tonight. I hoped they would support the Lit Club.

People milled everywhere, illuminated by the powerful overhead lights aimed at the field inside. When the aroma of fresh popcorn reminded me that I hadn't eaten since lunch, I stopped at the refreshment stand and bought a cup of cocoa for five dollars, which was highway robbery but contributed to the Stonedale booster club's fundraising efforts, so I wasn't going to complain.

Our school colors were crimson and silver; the other team's colors were black and gold. Fans were decked out in their team regalia to show spirit and support: Stonedale fans had a silver gryphon — our mascot — on their clothes, and the other team's fans had a golden lion on theirs. It all reminded me of medieval jousting competitions. Contributing even more to the illusion was a huge bonfire burning to the right of the stadium, surrounded by students holding cups and singing the university's fight song, which I recognized because the chancellor had played it for us at the beginning of the last mentoring meeting. Thankfully he hadn't made us sing along. A few of the voices belting out the lyrics this evening were adding a whimsical bit of drunken slurring.

I joined the outermost ring of the crowd, sipping my cocoa and soaking in the merriment all around me. Bit by bit, I edged through the throng of people. The group in front of me was yelling back and forth about the location of their seats in the stadium for what seemed like centuries. Finally, they left to find said seats, and I scored a space right next to the fire. The heat was absolutely delicious. I stretched out my free hand near the flames, trying to erase the chill. Suddenly, I was shoved from behind, towards the inferno.

CHAPTER 21

Twisting sharply to the left and rolling sideways prevented my death. I didn't even know my body could do that, I mused. Then sharp pain dragged me back into the immediacy of the moment. I had landed hard on the ground beside the fire, my hands taking the brunt of it. My palms were cut and bleeding. As I tried to determine the level of damage, a stinging sensation radiated up my arms as well. People swarmed around trying to be helpful, which hindered my ability to stand, and I remained on the cold ground in a daze for several moments. I was able to confirm that I wasn't burned, but my face was hot and my coat was covered with gray ash.

Finally, some kind strangers, cooing over my injuries like doves, helped me to my feet. I assured them that I was fine, but the whole thing had scared me senseless. At first I thought the crowd had simply surged forward, knocking me off balance, but the two students who had been standing behind me insisted someone in a hooded coat had squeezed in front of them, pushed me, and ran off.

"Could you see the person's face?" I asked the taller of the two young men. They both had their faces painted in Stonedale silver, and the effect was uncanny.

"No, dude. He blew past us and took off. Sorry."

Although part of me wanted to correct the application of "dude," I thanked them and hightailed it out of there.

Someone must have witnessed the bonfire episode because word got around fast. The phone rang all night long as colleagues and even the dean — which I considered a small miracle — left consoling messages. I let them all go to voicemail. All I wanted to do was sit on my sofa, drink tea, and stare at the television, on which was playing an old detective movie marathon. Perhaps not the best choice given the tenor of the day, but it was oddly soothing. I watched the handsome leading men and the glamorous leading ladies and tried to lose myself in a world where the bad guy always got caught, one way or another.

As soon as I had returned home, I looked up the Briar Rose Society online, but I hadn't found a single reference or link. I'd read through the original folktale of Little Briar Rose, but it hadn't provided any clues whatsoever. And somewhere along the way, I'd realized Simone still had my necklace.

I felt like a failure all around.

Cady curled up on the couch next to me and started purring as I petted her distractedly, wincing at the pressure — my wounded palms were excessively tender. I wished Calista would just explain the tattoo already. The fact that she had the symbol on her body was not only disturbing but, I felt sure, central to the strange happenings at Stonedale. If there was a secret society, as Simone had said, she must be a member. If she was a member, how far would she go to keep it a secret? Who else was a member? And what were they up to?

Struggling with the sense that I was missing a vital connection, I decided to go back to the beginning. I pulled out a legal pad and made a list of names, followed by reasons why they might have wanted to kill Roland.

Tad: angry about tenure
Elisabetta: angry about harassment

Willa: angry about bullying
Norton: wants to be chair

That was an unsatisfyingly short list. But the bigger problem was that none of those reasons would explain why Judith had been attacked, why Eldon had been killed, or why someone now appeared to be targeting me.

A loud knock at the front door echoed through my bungalow, interrupting my musings. Unwillingly, I pulled myself off of the sofa and checked through the peephole. Nate stood on my small porch. His red sweatshirt said "Lit Ninja," which made me like him that much more.

I held the door open and greeted him warmly.

He scanned me quickly from head to toe but didn't say anything. I walked into the kitchen, inviting him to make himself comfortable while I made another pot of tea.

Once we were settled on my sofa with mugs, Nate gave me a sympathetic look. "I thought you'd have bandages all over you. How are you doing?"

"Not great," I said, holding up my battered hands.

"What happened? All I heard was that you fell into the bonfire."

"I didn't fall in. I was pushed." I gave him

the particulars.

Nate appeared increasingly stunned as the story unfolded. "Why didn't you call me, Lila?"

"Don't know. Just wanted to hide, I guess."

"I don't think it's safe for you to be here alone."

I didn't think so either, truthfully.

Nate studied me, as if gauging something, and slid over slightly closer, his fresh soap scent surrounding me.

"How about if I stay here tonight?"

"I appreciate that, but then there's the next night, and the next. You can't just move in."

"Why don't you come to my apartment building? At least there's an alarm there."

I put my hand up to intervene. "I don't want to move out, and I don't want you to feel as though you have to be my bodyguard —"

"I don't mind," he said. "I don't want anything to happen to you, Lila."

"Thank you. But we need to find out who is doing these horrible things. That would solve the problem."

"That's true," he said. "It would."

It was quiet as we tried to figure out what to do next. "Have you spent much time in the basement of Crandall?" I asked.

He did a double take. "That's very left field. What are you talking about?"

I told him about the circular room and the meeting . . . or whatever that was.

"Have you told the detective any of that?"

"No. I'm not even sure what I saw down there. It did sound like there were multiple people involved, though. I'm certain of that much."

He leaned back and played with a spoon on the coffee table for a minute. His face was serious. "You should absolutely tell the detective."

"I don't know. It just sounds . . ." I fiddled with some pillow fringe.

"Crazy?"

"Yes."

"No one will think it's crazy if you catch someone doing something wrong. What do you think they're up to?"

"No idea. Plotting their next murder? Drinking blood? They might be devil worshippers for all I know."

"Maybe they were just . . . rehearsing a play?"

"I don't know," I said slowly. "They were chanting."

I was so glad to be able to talk this over with Nate, now that I'd told him everything else on Halloween. It felt productive to discuss it with someone rather than simply having the various pieces go around and around in my head all the time. "But I did get a clue, sort of. At the football game, Simone saw the thorn necklace and said it meant I'd been chosen for membership into the Briar Rose Society."

He perked up. "Explain, please."

I recounted the conversation I'd had with Simone.

"A secret society? Did you look them up online?"

"I did. Couldn't find a thing."

"Hence the secret part," he said gleefully.

"The initial letter that came with the thorn necklace definitely did not say anything about joining them. But my point is that maybe the society is the chanting group that meets in the basement?"

He pressed his hands together and rested them on his chin while he contemplated the information.

"Can you think back? Was there anything to identify them? Like a giant thorn ball hanging from the ceiling? Or a bunch of thorns lying around?"

"I couldn't see a thing. The door was only open partway to begin with, and when I got close, it slammed shut in my face. I don't even know if they knew I was there or what."

"Would you show me the necklace letters?" Nate asked.

"Sure," I said, reaching into my bag, which I'd stashed beneath the coffee table, and pulling out both. "But there isn't much to them."

He raised his eyebrows and settled back into the cushions to scan the letters.

"So the first one tells you to show the necklace to Calista, and the second one tells you to wear the necklace to the Halloween party."

"Correct."

"How are those two things connected?"

"No idea."

"And Calista wouldn't explain what the symbol is?"

"No. But I'm pretty sure she's involved. Somehow."

He looked thoughtful. "Has she ever committed a crime before?"

"Nate!" I stared at him. "Never. When I said 'involved,' I meant that she knows more than she's saying. Not that she's a *killer.*"

"I knew that," he said quickly, in response to my angry tone. "Just thinking out loud. Being thorough."

I went back to my satchel and withdrew the folder holding the Poe Collins articles.

"I also wanted to ask you about these. Will you take a look and see what you think?" I explained how I had found them.

Nate began reading. Cady jumped onto my lap, and I tried to refocus on the movie, though I had lost the thread of the plot.

After a few minutes, he put down the articles.

"These are weird," he said.

"What do you mean?" I turned to prop my elbow on the back of the sofa.

"They seem more intent upon tearing the authors down than they do on showing us something new about the books. Usually a good piece of literary criticism expands our reading possibilities, right? He — or she, I guess — basically just attacks the writer."

That was it in a nutshell. I don't know why the journals had seen fit to publish them. They were all newer journals, though, and content depended on the submissions received or lack thereof.

We tried to come up with reasons that the articles had been collected in a folder in the main office. The most logical explanation was that someone in our department had either been researching Poe Collins or had been writing as Poe Collins and was about to be taken to task for it.

Or maybe, though I didn't dare say this out loud, even killed for it.

CHAPTER 22

A week later, Nate and I were at Stonedale Correctional Facility, facing Tad through a thick cloudy window. As promised, Tad's father had made the necessary arrangements to allow us to visit quickly. I don't know how, and I didn't want to ask. We'd been ushered in by an unsmiling guard after having our credentials checked and our hands stamped with the same invisible ultraviolet code they used when I visited my cousin. Calista was meeting with her lawyer right now, so we weren't going to be able to see her as well, unfortunately. I certainly had a lot of questions for her.

Nate held the black phone up between our ears so we could both hear what Tad was saying. The thick metal cord attached to the wall on my side was therefore stretched across my neck. I tried not to think about the germs swarming over its surface.

"They charged me with killing Eldon and

as an accomplice to Roland's murder," said Tad. His five-o'clock shadow lent him an edgy air and his blond hair, normally groomed into a style that looked easy but probably took some work, stuck up in uneven lumps from his head.

"We know you didn't do anything," Nate said reassuringly.

At least we hoped he didn't.

"I was trying to pull the stake *out* of his chest, which put my prints on it and his blood all over me. The police find my story unconvincing, but wouldn't you try to remove the knife too, if it were you?"

"Depends," I said slowly. It hadn't even occurred to me to go near Roland's uncannily still body on the conference table.

"I thought he was still alive," Tad said. "I was trying to help him. But the stake was jammed in there, and the blood made it so slippery . . ."

I was glad he trailed off at that point. I took a deep breath to counter the sudden wobble in my stomach.

"And of course all the stuff with Roland last year supposedly provides motive," Tad continued. "As if I'd kill him for revenge, then his brother too for good measure? Who would *do* that?" He shook his head. "Even though Roland's gone, he's still ruining my life. Unbelievable."

"I'm sorry, man," said Nate quietly. He hadn't spoken much up to this point, which was unlike him. "What happens now?"

"Trial, though who knows when that will start," Tad said glumly, while examining, then brushing, something off of his sleeve. His bright orange prison jumpsuit appeared to be freshly pressed. I didn't know how he avoided wrinkles but they never seemed to plague him, even in jail.

I returned my attention to the conversation, where Nate was telling him about the people meeting in the basement.

Tad was thoughtful. "I don't know about any meetings, but there is an underground tunnel on campus."

"It's not just a rumor, then?" Nate leaned forward eagerly. "Does it link all of the buildings?"

"I don't know," Tad said. "But Crandall and Randsworth are definitely connected. My dad took me through once when I was young. We didn't go into any of the rooms, but I still thought it a fabulous adventure at the time, like exploring a catacomb." He snapped his fingers. "Oh, I also remember him telling my grandfather — also a Stonedale professor emeritus — that some controversial matters were being handled *circuitously.* In fact, he emphasized the word so much that I looked it up afterwards. At the time, I thought he meant there was a way to maneuver politically outside of meetings, but perhaps he meant there was a circular room where secret meetings were being held."

"That's got to be it." Nate elbowed me.

I nodded and asked Tad if he knew about any secret societies on campus.

"Just fraternities, sororities, and honor societies. That sort of thing. Is that what you mean?"

"Those are known. I'm talking about clandestine groups."

"No." He seemed genuinely baffled.

"Does the Briar Rose Society ring any bells?"

"Like in the folktale, where the woman is sleeping?" Tad asked.

"That's the one," I said. " 'Little Briar Rose.' It's a variant of 'Sleeping Beauty.' "

"No, sorry."

Nate and I exchanged a look. I didn't know what he was thinking, but I was considering the ways in which sleep sometimes figures metaphorically as death in literature. Was the Briar Rose Society responsible for the murders? That was an idea worth investigating.

"Is there anything we can do for you?" Nate asked Tad.

"My dad's team of legal eagles has descended upon Stonedale County Courthouse, so that's covered. But in the meantime, if you hear anything . . ."

"Consider it done," said Nate.

The following Tuesday, I ran into Nate by the department mailboxes in the main office. I beckoned him over. We'd talked for a long time after visiting Tad, and we both thought it was likely the society was behind the campus attacks. We had agreed to come up with plans for action individually.

"Do you have a plan yet?" I asked him.

"No," he said. "Wait, yes I do. We should tell the detective what's going on."

"I can't," I said. "If Calista's a member of the society, then I would be turning her in."

"True," he said. He pulled papers out of his mailbox and squinted inside to be sure he had gotten them all. "But if she's a killer, shouldn't she be turned in?"

"She's not a killer," I protested.

He tucked the papers into his bag, not saying anything.

"Can you meet me for coffee this afternoon?"

He shook his head. "No, I have advising

appointments."

"Then I'll just tell you my plan now. Let's see if we can figure out what's going on at those meetings. We could hide in the room where the books are stored tomorrow night and listen. I still have the key." Although I couldn't think of anything I wanted to do less than go back downstairs in the dark, I couldn't see a way around it.

His eyes lit up and he pointed at the basement. "Oh, you mean —"

"Yes. I don't know if they always meet at the same day and time."

"Let's find out," Nate said, decisively. "I'm in. Meet you in the stairwell at . . . when was it?"

"It was around six."

"Six? That doesn't seem like a very dastardly time to meet. I would have guessed midnight."

"Maybe they don't think anyone would bother them in their hidden location."

"You mean in their *evil lair.*"

I shot him a look. "Anyway, let's try to meet at quarter after five. I don't want to run into anyone else down there and —"

"Blow our cover?" He winked.

"Sure," I said. "Though I think we technically would need to *have* a cover before it could be blown." His lightheartedness was contagious, but inside I was afraid.

"Should I bring binoculars?" He was really getting into this.

"You can, but since we're going to be listening through a vent that doesn't open, all you'd see is the floor."

"Got it. But if this doesn't provide any answers, I'm going to Archer and telling him everything. It's just too dangerous around here."

I nodded.

He readjusted the strap of his backpack slung over one shoulder and gave me the little salute he favored. It was charming, as usual. "Talk to you later," he said loudly over his shoulder as he left, as if to throw off any eavesdropping bystanders.

Later that evening, I had reached the final paper in my current grading pile. This student clearly hadn't yet grasped the importance of a specific introduction, given that his essay began, "Since the dawn of time, great literature has been written." I could tell this one was going to require extensive commentary, an activity that necessitated a careful balance between encouragement and correction. Deep in the grading zone, I was startled by the sound of my cell phone ringing.

"Lila? It's Nate. I'm sorry to call so late, but I wanted to make sure we're ready for tomorrow."

"Yes, but . . . how do we protect ourselves? We aren't just exploring an empty tunnel. We're putting ourselves in the proximity of an unknown number of people who meet to do who knows what. It's not like the symbols are showing up in positive situations. It's probably not safe."

"Accurate on all counts." He paused. "But you won't be alone — and you can take some comfort in knowing that I regularly work out." He chuckled. "Right?"

His levity steadied me somewhat. "Yes, but —"

"I'll bring some mace too," he said. "Just in case."

I had no experience with weapons and wasn't sure if it would be better to bring something to protect us or to leave it behind. What if someone took it away from us and used it against us? The whole idea of violence made me queasy.

We said our goodbyes and I forced my attention back to that vague and rambling essay, wanting to restore at least some kind of order to the universe, however small.

I spent the night tossing and turning, worried about what would happen in the basement, and the next day passed in a blur. As a result, I didn't hear much of the chancellor's endless PowerPoint presentation on the university's plan for taking over the academic world, which called mostly for faculty to do a lot more work for the same amount of money. Or, as he called it, "Ten Steps to a Superior Stonedale." It was a bit of a shock when the overhead lights came back on. We all blinked sleepily before remembering to clap for the presentation, though most of us were probably applauding for its completion, not its content.

I had fifteen minutes until the rendezvous, and anxiety simmered just below the surface. Beneath the table, I unfolded the handwritten note I'd found in my mailbox after class and read it again: "Change in plan: Randsworth instead. Same time." I was glad Nate had realized that if we were lurking around at the bottom of the stairwell in Crandall, we might run into people going downstairs. It was much wiser to approach from the opposite end of the tunnel, now that we knew it went all the way to the other building. I'd chosen my wardrobe carefully this morning — dark clothing and flat shoes. If I had to run, I'd be prepared.

Finally, the mentor meeting was adjourned. I said goodbye to Judith and went to meet Nate at the appointed spot. The basement stairwell was empty, thankfully, but I still descended slowly, trying to be stealthy. No one was down there yet. As I waited near the doorway, I tried to ignore the tingle of apprehension ascending my spine. Perhaps I shouldn't be standing around in the light like a giant target.

After ten minutes, Nate still hadn't arrived. I was going to have to do this without him if I didn't want to run into anybody in the hallway. I pushed through the fire door and crept carefully down the dark corridor towards the place where it curved, hoping the door of the circular room was closed enough for me to sneak by and get into the storage room without being seen. As I paused to pull the key out of my bag, I heard a sound behind me and whirled around.

In a flash, a figure was upon me, striking me on the head, and I felt myself sliding into darkest shadow.

CHAPTER 23

I awoke to find myself inside an unfamiliar room, with a pile of dissected student desk parts — chair legs protruding from the heap at unnatural angles — taking up the far half of the space. A wall of empty metal shelves was directly across from me. The single light bulb hanging crookedly down from the ceiling was on, though it seemed better at accentuating the gloom than providing illumination. It appeared to be a different storage room from the one I'd been aiming for.

This was bad. Very bad. At least I was still on campus, which was slightly comforting given that I could have been in a ditch somewhere right now. But I didn't want to meet my end in a student-desk graveyard either.

I stood up slowly and made my way over to the door. I jiggled the knob, but it was locked tight. Pounding on the wood and yelling for help only caused lightning to streak across my brain from the spot where I'd been hit.

I gently pressed the bump at the side of my head to gauge the discomfort — about an eight out of ten on the pain scale — and tried to come up with a plan. I reached into my pocket with the other hand, but my cell phone was gone.

Shakily, I sank to the floor.

A sound coming from a vent on the wall to my right drew my attention. I crawled over and adjusted it — thankfully, this one wasn't stuck — until I could see into the next room, where about thirty people were filing silently in. Each came to a stop before one of the chairs facing the wooden podium, but they did not sit down. Whoever had knocked me out must have dragged me into the storage room on the opposite side of the circular room where I'd heard the chanting.

It was difficult to tell from this low side angle who they were. What the heck was going on?

Someone stepped up to a podium and faced the crowd. She opened a red book, from which she read in a dramatic manner. With shock, I recognized Willa's voice. At certain points, the audience would respond, sounds of affirmation or denial, as in a religious service. Or, I shuddered, a darker ceremony.

Her voice rang out. "Greetings, sisters."

"Greetings," replied the crowd.

"Please take a seat." As they complied, Willa continued. "Join me, sisters," she said. "We meet here . . ."

"In the tomb," said the crowd.

"Where so many have been left . . ."

"Unsung," voiced the crowd.

Willa produced a large knife from somewhere and held it up, point side down. Then she made a fierce stabbing motion. "We vow . . ."

"Vow!" repeated the crowd.

"To celebrate those who came before. We promise to sever" — another stab — "the old ways and nurture new ones. We renew this vow with every gathering of the Briar Rose Society. If you agree, please affirm."

"Secrecy for truth," said the crowd.

When Willa made another violent slice through the air, I lurched backwards, hitting something behind me, which made a noise as it scraped across the floor. One of the individuals in the row closest to me turned her head sharply over her shoulder. I froze until she faced front. I assumed one or more of the group members had dragged me in here, and I didn't want them coming to hit me on the head a second time.

Scenarios ran unbidden through my mind, starting with Roland's murder. If Willa had approached Roland from the front, where the knife had entered his body, he could have stopped her. Unless he didn't see the knife coming. Could they have been embracing? But if she had been so ill-treated by him, as Calista claimed, that wouldn't have happened. Or was their behavior intended to cover a romantic relationship? Hard to imagine. But I had just seen her demonstrate a stabbing in front of a room full of people . . . that seemed fairly damning, didn't it? Not to mention terrifying.

There was a beat of stillness, then a hand in the front row was raised. "I move . . ." I couldn't hear the rest of the sentence.

"I second," came a voice from the back.

A vote was taken and declared successful.

As I listened, I became increasingly light-headed. I knew I was going to faint and tried to fight it but a loud roaring filled my ears, and I slowly slid forward.

I awakened on the floor some time later to absolute quiet.

Scuttling over to the wall, I checked through the vent again. The room was empty and the lights were off, so I couldn't see anything. I stood very slowly and tried to figure out what to do next.

There were footsteps in the hallway.

My whole body vibrated with adrenaline. I ran over to the desk parts pile and grabbed a dismembered chair leg to use as a weapon, then crouched down behind the shelves, trying to make myself invisible. I peeked through the metal bars.

When the door flew open, Willa was standing there.

Freakin' Willa. Madam Big Knife Herself.

Then another woman entered, holding a red book. It was Judith. *Judith?* I couldn't accept it.

Strangely, they didn't seem to be looking for me. They just glided in soundlessly. It gave me goosebumps.

My mind raced. There were two murderers here. I didn't think I could fight them both at once. Maybe the best I could hope for was that whatever they had in mind was quick and painless.

Then another person came through the door. My odds were getting worse by the second.

Millicent was holding the knife I'd seen Willa using in one hand and a small black gun in the other. She swept the room with her eyes, calling my name.

I didn't move.

"Lila, if you don't come out here, I'll shoot Judith right now."

I crept out from my hiding spot, chair leg in hand.

"Drop it," she said. "If you throw that at me, I'll shoot you. Now join the others, over by the wall."

I did as she said.

"Sit down, ladies," she ordered. "And put that book on the floor, Judith."

We all complied with Millicent's directions as she watched, weapons aimed unwaveringly at us.

I didn't understand why she was turning on her accomplices, who both seemed terribly pale.

Millicent's eyes glittered. "No funny stuff. I am happy to use this knife or shoot this gun. Either one works for me."

"Who hit me?" My question came out as a croak. I was trying desperately to come up with an escape plan but couldn't work out how to do anything without getting shot.

"Be quiet," Willa, sitting next to me, whispered.

"I'm surprised your brain still works after the crack from my pistol here," Millicent said. "You're stronger than I'd thought."

"Let us go," Willa said. "You don't have to

do this."

Wait, they weren't in this together?

"Oh, yes I do," Millicent said, briskly. "But first, let's review, so I'm sure you all understand your sins."

Judith spoke quietly. "I'm sorry, Millicent. Spencer is a very special man, and I understand how you might resent me for —"

"What? You think I want your husband? How ridiculous. And completely wrong." Millicent leaned against the wall, smug as a cat. "I don't hate you because of Spencer, Judith. It's because of Betty. More specifically, the way the members of your group treated Betty."

"She told you about the Briar Rose Society?" Judith said, sounding surprised.

"She founded the whole thing —"

Willa interrupted. "That's not quite true. We were involved too."

Millicent waved her hand dismissively. "You helped her, sure. But it was her idea. She's a genius."

"But she told you about it?" Judith asked again, openly incredulous. "The first thing we agreed on was that members needed to keep it a secret."

"She didn't so much tell me directly as she did write about it in her journals," said Millicent. "Which I always read when I house-sat for her. So, clearly, she wanted me to know."

That was some twisted logic right there.

"What exactly is the society?" I asked, seizing my opportunity. I couldn't seem to tie the pieces together, but I had to know.

"We were going to invite you to join, Lila," said Willa.

"Why would I want to join a society that kills people?"

"What? No, that's not what we do," said Judith, shaking her head. "Why would you think that?"

"Let's see — there was the rose symbol on the knife that killed Roland, for starters," I said.

"That was me," said Millicent proudly. "Using the society's original ritual knife."

"And on the stake that killed Eldon —" I continued.

"Also me, though I made that one myself," Millicent chimed in again. She appeared to have no qualms about knocking off whoever crossed her path. It was chilling, how pleased she was about her evil deeds.

"How did you get the ritual knife?" Willa asked in clipped tones. I could tell she was angry but trying to control it. "Calista was taking over as president, but I can't believe she would have let it out of her sight."

"I saw it in Calista's office when I went in to leave a desk copy that had arrived for her. She was in class. I would have preferred to use my gun, but there was a poetic quality to framing the Briar Rose Society after what you did to my sister."

"What do you mean, what the society did to your sister?" Judith asked.

"Once Betty retired from the university, you forgot about her. You should have seen her, lying around her apartment like a broken doll."

"She told us she wanted some space after Nala died." Judith spoke calmly.

"Wasn't Nala the name of Elisabetta Vega's partner?" I was confused.

Millicent glowered. "Yes. And Elisabetta will always be Betty to me."

"Wait," I said. "Elisabetta is your *sister*?"

"Yes, my sister. Everyone knows that. You really need to get up to speed, Lila." Millicent looked sharply at Judith. "Betty and I are very close. Sisterhood might not mean anything to you other than a handy political slogan, but it does to me."

"We love her, Millicent," said Willa angrily.

"But you abandoned her."

"No, we didn't," Judith said, a pained expression on her face.

I was still trying to process the sibling connection. "But you have different last names."

"And different fathers," Millicent said. "Doesn't make us any less related."

Half-sisters, then. Perhaps that accounted for why they didn't resemble each other in the least.

"But . . ." I began, pausing to attempt to sort out my thoughts.

"Yes?" Millicent asked, snapping her fingers. "Out with it."

"Why did you want to kill Roland in the first place?"

"It was a combination of things, really," Millicent said, fixing me with a thoughtful gaze. "I didn't plan to kill anyone, but once I started, I found I had quite a knack for it."

So disturbing.

"I suppose it wouldn't hurt to tell you. Since you're not walking out of here alive."

I started to shiver.

"As you know, Betty was up for professor emerita status. Roland wrote a horrible memo outlining the reasons why she didn't deserve it and asked me to make copies for the meeting to hand out to the entire department. It would have humiliated her."

"That's terrible," Judith said. Her hands were shaking, but her voice was even.

"It is. I destroyed it. But on the same day,

he . . . well, he asked me to submit something else that would have libeled my sister. And I was having none of that."

Light dawned so hard that it made my head ache.

"Does your sister write mysteries?"

A repellent smirk spread across Millicent's face. "I knew you'd figured it out."

"What are you talking about?" Willa interjected.

Millicent gestured with the gun. "Go ahead, Professor."

I put my palms onto the floor to steady myself. The laser beam of hate she sent my way was dizzying.

"Did you know Elisabetta writes mysteries?" I addressed my colleagues.

"Yes," said Willa. "As Eve Turner. But only a few of us know."

"They're superb," said Millicent. "Extremely smart and sophisticated."

"I think so too, actually," Willa agreed politely, as if we were all sitting at book club, sipping tea together, which only intensified the surreal quality of the moment.

"But what do her books have to do with Roland?" Judith asked.

I tried to think of a way to explain without setting Millicent off. I opted for my calmest teacher voice and addressed my fellow captives. "Are you familiar with Poe Collins?"

I heard Millicent mutter something about a "ridiculous pen name."

My colleagues seemed confused. Both were shaking their heads.

"He's a literary critic who has published several articles recently, but I could only find two at our library. From what I could tell, Collins's thing was to choose specific authors and write scathing articles about why . . . um . . ." I glanced at Millicent. "Do you want to explain?"

"Go on," she commanded.

"About why, in his opinion, they were failures."

Willa and Judith glanced at each other.

Millicent jumped in at that point. "His latest article savaged my sister's work. In its entirety. He gave it me to proofread and submit to the journal for him, as he always did. I don't even know if he was aware that it was Betty he was attacking, but it didn't matter." She made a face. "I was having no more of Roland Higgins. I've hated him for years, but this was the last straw. I knew he would be the first at the department meeting — he was always so concerned about staking out the best chair for his fat ass — so I took a chance he'd be alone in the room and went to stop him."

"You were protecting Liz," Judith said soothingly. "I understand."

"You understand nothing," Millicent snarled. "It was more than protection. I wanted revenge for every horrible thing he ever did to her. From the harassment forward. I'm talking about *real* revenge, not like those Briar edition books you think will have such momentous impact. Though one did come in handy when it was time to hit you, Judith."

"Ah," said Judith. I admired her composure under the circumstances.

"I read that ritual book too," Millicent said, sneering at the red volume next to Judith. "You overanalyzed every single element of your stupid little group, didn't you? Though you appear to have overlooked the part where Briar Rose was awakened by the kiss of a man."

Willa made a sound of disgust, and her voice was harsh. "We don't have anything against men. Just against the silencing of women. And haven't *you* overlooked the fact that your own sister was part of the planning Judith just described? You say you've done all of this on her behalf, yet you're mocking her work. Are you completely soulless?"

"I hope that's the case, considering what I've done," said Millicent. "And what I'm about to do."

My teeth began chattering slightly. It took concentration to make them stop.

"After it was over, I was delighted to have dispatched of Roland. It awakened something in me, I'll confess."

"Why did you attack Judith?" Willa demanded.

"I was trying to frame you, remember? I hoped you'd start to suspect each other. No one seemed to be talking about the symbol on the knife, so I had to get another one circulating out there. So I brought Betty's embossed copy of the Woolf book and waited until Judith was alone."

She produced a laugh that sounded like a demented bird screeching in a horror movie. "Then I learned Eldon had co-written the Poe Collins articles. If I didn't stop him, he'd publish the article on Betty's work." Millicent sighed dramatically. "Though even if he hadn't been a co-author, I probably would have killed him anyway. Having Eldon around was like Roland coming back to life. Couldn't have that. I'd run out of holy society relics by then, so I had to whittle my own stake."

She *whittled* a stake and carved the symbol

320

on it? That was dedication. I suppose there were no lengths to which she wouldn't go, given her singularity of purpose.

"Was that you who destroyed my office too?"

"Yes," she said. "I was hoping the symbols in your office might prompt some conversation about the society with the detective. I made sure they were colossal. Impossible to ignore. You know, clues for dummies."

"I did talk about the symbols with the detective, but they were all pointing to my cousin," I said, fighting a flare of anger. "I didn't know they came from a society."

"Way to connect the dots. I thought you were smarter than that," Millicent scoffed. "You'd already received Betty's necklace I sent you. Didn't Calista tell you about the society when you wore it to see her?"

"No. She told me to hide it. She must have known that no current society member would have given it to me."

"Then how did you find out about the society?"

"From Simone," I said. "She saw the necklace and thought it meant I'd been invited to join."

"What?" Willa seemed perplexed. "How did she know about us?"

"Her mother belonged to the society when

she was here," Judith reminded her.

"It's a pity she couldn't keep her mouth shut." Willa addressed me. "We all take a vow of secrecy. That's why none of us could explain anything to you."

Millicent rolled her eyes. "Well, I'll admit it was harder than I thought it would be to frame the society . . . because most people didn't know it existed. Should have thought that through."

"Were you also the one who pushed me into the bonfire?"

"Yes," she said. "The second note told you to wear the necklace to the Halloween party, and you defied me. Punishment was in order. Plus, by then, I was just plain aggravated by the sight of you. But let's cut to the chase here, shall we? I did everything. All of it." Millicent sounded triumphant. "Laughing the whole time at how ridiculous you all are, thinking you could change history."

Judith spoke up. "We just wanted to claim a space for women who have not been able to speak their truths. Like you, Millicent."

Millicent trained her gun on Judith. "Do not presume to know anything about *me*. It might interest you to know I have a far higher IQ than Betty. Probably higher than all of you. To be blunt, I could smash your precious literary interpretations to smithereens without even trying. All you professors think you're so smart, but oh, how easy it was to fool you. Almost got annoying by the end, how slow you were." She cleared her throat and addressed me directly. "Speaking of idiots, aren't you wondering where your boyfriend is, Lila?"

"Do you mean Nate?"

"Yes. He's probably waiting for you at your house right now. I put a note in his mailbox cancelling your plans. It wasn't very bright of you to make arrangements in the main office . . . I could hear every word you said. From there, it was simply a matter of dividing and conquering." Millicent laughed. "It was very helpful of Tad to get arrested too. Now he can take the blame for everything. Or he and Calista can split it. I couldn't care less."

"Well, I care," I said, furious. "What makes you think any of this is fair?"

"Fair?" Millicent glared at me. "Life is never fair, Professor."

The anger coursing through my body was preferable to the fear. My thinking seemed more focused somehow. I ran through a few escape scenarios in my mind, but they all ended with Millicent shooting someone.

"Please, Millicent, why don't you let us

go? We won't say anything," said Willa. Her coaxing tone provided an odd contrast to the steely look in her eyes. "Think about it. You could walk away right now and leave town. As you just said, Tad or Calista will take the blame."

"And miss all the fun after your bodies are discovered? I don't think so." She sounded almost merry. She would enjoy killing us. I tried to catch one of the other women's eyes in a desperate attempt to telegraph something, anything, that might spark a plan.

Willa spoke up again. "There's got to be something you want, Millicent. Could we make a deal?"

"What I want," Millicent said coldly, "is to make you suffer for ignoring my sister in her time of need. If you hadn't —"

"We never ignored her," said Judith evenly. "She and I speak weekly, and she has been invited to all society events."

"But you didn't come to visit her much after Nala died. I was the only one there for her, same as it's been our whole lives. I may be the younger sister, but I'm much stronger, in every way. Actions speak louder than words."

"We were respecting her privacy," Willa

said. "She told us she wanted to be alone to grieve."

"Well, you didn't *believe* her, did you?" Millicent was clearly incensed. "You could have tried harder." She cocked the gun and aimed it at Willa's head. "Now you will pay for that."

"Wait," said Willa, arms out before her, as if that would shield her from the bullets.

The sound of running feet in the hallway made us all turn towards the door.

A moment later, Millicent tumbled backward, her weapons clattering on the cement.

The ritual book dropped with a thud onto the floor soon afterwards.

We scrambled to our feet. Willa, pale but resolute, went over and stood next to the unconscious Millicent to make sure she stayed put.

I stared at Judith. "You saved us."

"Must admit, that was very satisfying," she said, though she was trembling.

"But you only had one chance to hit her with the book!" I exclaimed.

"Indeed." Judith smiled. "We're lucky it worked."

"Now that's *real* poetic justice," Willa mused. "Don't you think?"

Suddenly, Nate jumped into the doorway, his body landing in some kung-fu-esque pose. He was dressed in black and had a flashlight dangling from his belt.

"Thanks, but we have things under control," Willa informed him.

He stood up and let his hands fall to his sides as he looked around, obviously confused.

As the other women started to fill him in on what had happened, Nate headed straight over to where I was standing.

And kissed me.

For a long time.

"Wha— what was that?" I asked, astonished.

"I don't know," he said, seeming equally surprised. "Let's revisit it later."

CHAPTER 24

On Friday morning, I sat at a small table in the crowded student union with the other women who had survived The Millicent Ordeal, including Calista. The gently falling snow visible through the large windows added a tranquil backdrop to the scene.

What a difference a week makes.

It had taken several days to suspend the images cascading nonstop through my mind. Police swarming in, guns drawn and grim. Millicent, waking to discover herself cuffed and in the custody of officers, emitting bloodcurdling screams. Willa and Judith, blankets around their shoulders, talking with the paramedics. Detective Archer taking down my description of events as I held an icepack to my throbbing head. At least this time he was no longer looking at me with suspicion. Thank goodness for that.

Judith had just invited us all over for Thanksgiving dinner when Calista interrupted, "Sorry, but I have to know before we talk about anything else . . . Millicent's in jail, right?" Her cheeks, bright from the cold, just about matched her hot pink sweater. She clutched the mug of tea in front of her as if absorbing strength from it.

"Yes. Tad's out, she's in, and they charged her with the murders, so as long as the trial goes well, she'll be there for a very long time," said Judith, turning her small gold watch around her wrist as she spoke.

Millicent deserved to be locked up for life in a tiny gray cell. But poor Elisabetta. I couldn't imagine what it felt like to have a sister like that, who had done so many terrible things supposedly on her behalf.

Calista smiled. "That's wonderful news. And I have more. Spencer just gave me a copy of his letter recommending tenure. It still has to go up through the different levels, but it's very supportive — unlike Roland's."

We all cheered.

"And how are we doing today?" Judith asked, making eye contact with each of us individually. Her stunning white hair was becomingly gathered into a long braid, which provided a striking contrast to her deep burgundy jacket.

"I'm fine," I said, though it came out

sounding more like a question than a declaration. I was still a little shaky.

Willa was more decisive. "Absolutely perfect." She readjusted her amethyst wool wrap and straightened up. "Ready to move on."

Calista agreed. "But first . . ." She groped around in her giant canvas bag, pushing aside books and papers, then made a sound of triumph and presented me with a small red box topped with a mauve ribbon. "This is for you, Lil."

"What's this? I didn't know we were giving gifts. It's not Christmas yet."

"Open it," she commanded.

I carefully removed the paper and lifted up the lid. Nestled inside was a necklace on a chain — the Briar Rose symbol engraved on a silver disc.

I looked up at Calista, puzzled.

"We're disbanding the society," she said. "But we wanted you to know we think of you as an honorary member."

"I'm flattered," I said. "I wish I could have participated. I think. I mean, it seems like everyone I know is a member, but I still don't know what the society was for."

"Well, in truth, you still can participate," said Judith. "We're going to come aboveground, as it were, and form a brand new group devoted to the study of women's literature through the department."

"Wait, it was a literary society?" I had been so far off of the mark. "How did it begin?"

"As a women's support group, initially. Liz and I had been involved in something similar in grad school, and it just seemed natural to start one here. The society has been active at Stonedale for several decades now. In addition to helping each other solve workplace-related issues, part of our purpose was to create an alternative canon, to foreground women writers we thought had been overlooked or unfairly disparaged. Lately, we've been experimenting with starting our own press, so we bound together mockups named after our favorite authors to see what might be involved and whether it was sustainable. We were going to call them Briar editions and emboss them with the society seal."

"The ones you saw were not for public consumption," Willa said. "The words inside were placeholder gibberish, not the actual texts."

"Yes," Judith agreed. "These were just examples — meant to circulate privately among society members. There was one additional book with our ritual language, which Calista had bound when she did the others."

"That's the one you threw at Millicent?"

"The very one."

"I'm so grateful for that book. And for your excellent aim."

Judith smiled at me.

"So why was it called the Briar Rose Society?" I asked her.

"We thought Briar Rose or Sleeping Beauty was symbolically evocative of the oppression women writers had experienced —"

"The thorny branches," I murmured.

"Yes, and she also embodied a sense of awakening that we hoped to champion. Putting the emblem on the ritual knife was representative of cutting ties with the traditional canon."

"I'm glad you went with Briar Rose," Calista said. "The Sleeping Beauty Society sounds like a never-ending makeover party."

We laughed.

"How many people belong to the society?" I asked.

"About forty professors from across campus. All of the women in our department were members — except for you and Simone," said Judith. "We make it a rule not to approach anyone until they've been here at least a full semester. New assistant professors have enough to deal with right away. We would have invited you next term."

"Makes sense —" I began, but Calista interrupted me with an apologetic expression.

"That's why I couldn't say anything." she said, squeezing my arm. "Members are sworn to secrecy, and I took that seriously. The knife was Elisabetta's — she gave it to me when she retired. I knew if I said it was hers, people would think she had something to do with Roland. I didn't want to get her in any trouble. And I transferred the knife symbol into a graphic as a way to . . . I don't know . . . celebrate us. Signal solidarity. Once I recreated it as a digital file, we could use it all over the place. Members were given necklaces, and it just seemed natural to emboss the Briar editions when we started making them. But in any case, forgive me for not being able to tell you before."

"Forgiven," I reassured her.

"Also, when you came to the jail and showed me the necklace, I knew something was wrong. There was no way you would have been given one since you weren't initiated yet. And I knew we weren't inviting new members until spring. So someone was trying to get you arrested too or trying to send me a message, but I didn't know what it was."

"I didn't know either. It was weird how everything seemed potentially meaningful but didn't add up to anything. For example, what were you and Willa arguing about at your party, Judith?"

"We were strategizing about the drama course syllabus she wanted to pass. We weren't angry at each other . . . just anxious about the matter at hand, I suppose."

"I see. Okay, and now for the big question: why did you meet down in that extremely creepy basement?"

All of the women laughed.

"We simply wanted to keep a low profile for the group and that was the only place we knew about where we wouldn't be disturbed," said Judith. "When we first conceived of the society, we were very passionate about creating an appropriate sense of community for our work —"

"A sacred space," clarified Willa.

"Precisely," said Judith. "We knew, of course, about other societies that used costumes — robes, hoods, and so forth — to immerse their members in the experience. We didn't want to go quite that far, but we did develop elements that made sense to us at the time, like the symbol, which was inspired by an old woodcut of the folktale. The knife was simply ceremonial and metaphorical."

"Until Millicent came along," said Calista, frowning.

Judith nodded. "She truly believed she was Liz's protector. You know, I do remember Liz mentioning a few strange things that happened while they were growing up . . . Millicent may always have had obsessive tendencies."

"It's especially bizarre considering Liz is entirely capable of taking care of herself," Calista said. "She's one of the strongest people I know."

"Yes, but it wasn't only about protection," said Willa. "It was about their relationship as sisters. Millicent saw us as a threat. She would have done *anything* to remain the most important person in Liz's life."

We fell quiet for a moment.

Judith addressed me. "Have you seen the statue between Crandall and Randsworth?"

"The veiled woman? Yes," I said. "She's beautiful. Kind of sad, though."

"Many years ago, Liz and I found her at an antique store and fell in love with her instantly. She seemed to represent all the women writers we were fighting for, so we spirited her on campus in the middle of the night. The school newspaper did a story about the statue, then it was picked up by the news wire and, well, we became a national mystery. No one at Stonedale could figure out where she came from."

I smiled at her.

Judith continued. "I don't know if you noticed, but she is located directly over the underground meeting room. She was our symbol of being visible and invisible at the same time."

"Secrecy for truth," Willa added with a shrug.

"No more secrecy," said Calista happily. "Just truth. Which is a lot easier to remember."

The last faculty meeting of fall term was blessedly uneventful.

First on the agenda was an update on the crimes. Spencer described our ordeal in some detail, apologized for Millicent's behavior, and thanked Judith, Willa, Calista, Nate, Tad, and me for our "bravery, both past and future," as he put it. We had all been subpoenaed to testify at the upcoming trial. He was sure, he said, that Millicent would be convicted several times over.

Reports were invited, and Norton treated

us to a twenty-minute play-by-play of the assessment project. I don't know if a single person in the room could have identified his main point, but when he sat down, we all applauded courteously.

Simone reported on the recent efforts of the Literature Club, somehow making her own participation sound like the vital key to their success, and smiled prettily as expressions of gratitude were extended her way. She studiously avoided my gaze afterwards, I noticed. Judith announced the launch of a new scholarly group focused on the study and preservation of women's literature. Suggestions for a name would be taken at the first meeting. She invited everyone to become a member and added that she hoped I would consider co-chairing.

Simone pursed her lips at that.

Spencer reminded us that exams would end the first week of December. He also encouraged us to suggest candidates for the executive assistant and Renaissance literature positions, if we had anyone in mind. "And since we won't have another department meeting until January, I'd like to take this opportunity to wish you all a very safe and a very pleasant winter break — which should not begin until after you submit final grades, of course."

There were polite chuckles all around.

Nate, sitting next to me, jabbed me with his elbow. "Hey, you made it through your first semester," he whispered.

"Barely," I whispered back.

"But you made it." He grinned at me, his blue eyes crinkling up rather adorably at the corners.

Maybe I did belong here at Stonedale after all.

ABOUT THE AUTHOR

Cynthia Kuhn is professor of English at MSU Denver, where she teaches literature and writing. Her work has appeared in *McSweeney's Quarterly Concern, Literary Mama, Copper Nickel, Prick of the Spindle, Mama, PhD* and other publications; she also blogs with Mysteristas. The first book in the Lila Maclean series received a William F. Deeck-Malice Domestic Grant.

The employees of Thorndike Press hope you have enjoyed this Large Print book. All our Thorndike, Wheeler, and Kennebec Large Print titles are designed for easy reading, and all our books are made to last. Other Thorndike Press Large Print books are available at your library, through selected bookstores, or directly from us.

For information about titles, please call:
(800) 223-1244

or visit our website at:
gale.com/thorndike

To share your comments, please write:
Publisher
Thorndike Press
10 Water St., Suite 310
Waterville, ME 04901